Mind of A Neighbor

by Lynn Hobbs

Book 3 of 3 in the:
American Neighborhood Series

Mind of a Neighbor

By Award Winning Author:
Lynn Hobbs

Proof Productions
Karnack, Texas

Mind of a Neighbor
Copyright©2022 by Lynn Hobbs

Cover art by Jeff Brannon
Proof Productions

PRINTED IN THE UNITED STATES OF AMERICA

ISBN-13: 979-8-218-09184-2
ISBN-10: 979-8-218-09184-2

Dedication

First of all, I want to give God the glory for His guidance with this book, and its completion. At times it seemed impossible this last book in the series would ever be written. Many interruptions, necessary new priorities, and life-changing surprises that I faced strengthened my faith and drew me closer in relationship with our Heavenly Father. I highly recommend reading the Bible daily and unlearning pagan traditions.

I thank God for the encouragement, help, and time given by my son, Jeff Brannon, in editing and publishing this book, and for my son, Mike Brannon, who has been super supportive as well.

Chapter One

"I feel guilty leaving Houston."

"We all do, Kate." Ethan's face softened listening to his wife. Driving from the city shelter after gathering their salvageable belongings had been an ordeal in itself. This particular shelter would soon be closing. Evacuees felt panic at the new crisis. Their departure today had been the last resort.

The destruction by Hurricane Harvey engulfed them in a sadness that seemed to grow deeper with each mile. Two weeks earlier, they had endured high winds, sixty plus inches of rain, flooding in all directions, no electricity, and no food. A normal way of life seemed to be impossible. After help had arrived, homes were gutted or condemned, and volunteer disaster teams were a lifesaver to thousands. Neighbors realized the horrific and painful long-term impact on themselves and their city. They kept discussing options, and none of them worked.

"How can FEMA expect us to pay back a low-interest loan?"

Ethan glanced in the rear-view mirror at their neighbor, Sal Hernandez.

"Sal, I can't answer that. I guess they have good intentions. Recent statistics prove they are helping many desperate people in a hopeless situation."

"Could you pay it back, Ethan?"

"No. I'm making payments on a house scheduled to be

condemned. My truck that is underwater still has to be paid for."

"I'm obligated to pay each month on my house, truck, and car; and can't use any of them." Sal's voice broke as he stared out the side window. "Most everyone I know didn't have flood insurance."

"Unfortunately, we had recently bought a new washer and dryer." His wife Maria added.

Ethan nodded.

Kate whispered to Ethan. "And that's why we help each other. We could be that family sitting in the back seat. That could even be our little kids."

Ethan's voice was barely audible. "It's the Christian thing to do, and they have no other means of evacuation."

Kate turned to make eye contact with Maria. Sal, Maria, and their children, Carlos and Rosa sat awkwardly in the back seat. The children lay sprawled with Ethan's dog, Rufus. A thought of innocence towards the children crossed her mind, and her heart broke at the family's vulnerable situation. Reassuring them as well as herself, Kate's face softened with a slow, confident smile. She haltingly patted Maria's knee.

"Starting over in a country farmhouse sounds cozy."

"I'm glad it's available, and you offered to share it." Maria's bottom lip quivered, and Kate realized how much strength they all needed.

"We are united in Christ. I believe what we're doing is His will."

"And if it lines up with His Word, then it is His will." Sal leaned forward with a sudden bright-eyed happiness. "Ethan, tell us about this farmhouse we're all thankful for."

"Well, I think you'll like it. It's my birthplace. My inheritance from my parents. A rambling two-story house: it is miles from the nearest neighbor. Has a wraparound porch, and three bedrooms, and I don't know how many bathrooms were added. Most of the rooms are now large; kitchen, dining room, living room, den, and a screened-in area in the backyard with a firepit. They remodeled a year before Dad passed away. Mom lived on for another year. She missed him dearly." He sighed. "I have fond memories there."

"I like our destination." Sal slowly settled back in the seat wiggling to get comfortable. Placing his hands behind his head, he appeared relaxed for the first time since the trip began.

"And I feel like we can do this. With God's guidance, our combined families can work together."

"Me too." Maria snuggled against her husband. "Wake us when we're there."

"I will in about 15 hours." Ethan winked with amusement.

"Sure you will." Sal laughed. "The way I feel, I think I could sleep for fifteen hours."

Ethan continued driving the Chevy Suburban while the others napped off and on. Getting a late start had been unavoidable. Ethan and Sal loaded the U-Haul trailer days ago, but last-minute packing of daily personal items seemed to take forever. Everyone had to use something again before it could be re-packed. Alarms woke them at 6 am. Their plan to leave immediately after an early breakfast at 7 a.m. didn't happen, though. They left Houston at nine o'clock in the morning.

"Oh!" Ethan flinched as Kate poked him in his side. "You're awake."

"And alert." She beamed. "Thought you could use help driving. I volunteer."

"Do you, now? I could welcome your offer, or I could drive from Texas to Kansas in the shortest time ever. Might set a record." He straightened his posture and stifled a laugh.

"No record today. Maybe another day."

They exchanged darting glances.

"I'll help drive." Sal interrupted.

Maria shifted her weight in the seat, opened her eyes, and yawned.

"Help with what?"

"Driving."

"Sounds like a plan. Let's do it."

"Stop at the next rest area and I'll drive." Kate took a deep, satisfied breath. "I'm anxious to get to Kansas now."

"We need to stop for lunch anyway."

Ethan found a truck stop nearby on the GPS.

Rufus exited the car first, and quickly got his business over with. Windows were lowered to provide air circulation, and Ethan locked Rufus back into the vehicle.

The meal proved to be exceptional. After restroom trips and filling the car with another full tank of gas, Kate drove.

The trip continued in silence; each passenger presumably lost in their own thoughts. Hours later dusk gave way to a night surrounding them in total darkness. Kate counted road marker signs under her breath. A calmness seemed to hang in the air as the Chevy continued a journey filled with hope. Ethan snored softly as he sprawled in the passenger seat.

No one stirred behind her, and she felt her hands relax from their grip on the steering wheel.

But the immediate past crept upon her again, and she tensed as visions of Houston's destruction quickly flooded her mind. Piles of ruined furniture and soaked wet insulation mingled with soggy mattresses, muddy clothes, unusable picture frames, odd pieces of lumber stuck out that had formerly upheld a home, and broken dishes. All were thrown together in a continuous row along the sides of each road where trees and other debris clung to the landscape like an ugly mountain of ruin. Personal items were displayed haphazardly by the water for all to view. She shuddered as the memory played out like a rerun of a horror movie she didn't want to watch, yet there it played again. Kate quietly prayed for her other neighbors who went to live with relatives in other parts of the state, and for Brother Williford, their pastor, who had bonded with everyone in the church.

She sighed deeply remembering the difficulty of saying final goodbyes. A strong church family, they vowed to keep in contact with each other.

A thickness grew in her throat, signaling the onset of tears. Her shoulders slumped as she emitted another heavy sigh.

"You okay?" Ethan lightly squeezed her arm.

"Hmm? Yes." Kate took in the comfortable warmth of his face and felt her tension dissolve. "I… I am remembering…"

"You don't have to explain." He squeezed her arm again. Now wide awake, he sat upright. "I can drive."

"No, I am fine. Guess it got overwhelming again."

"We're in this together."

Kate flashed him a quick smile. "We better be."

He tilted back his head. "Oh, we are in it for the long haul."

Sal's voice sailed out from the back seat. "Hey, we're in it for the long haul, too."

Kate smiled as she drove through a well-lit country town.

Carlos and Rosa wiggled out of their parent's laps and looked out the window.

Ethan leaned over the headrest and made eye contact with Sal in the back seat. Grinning, he spoke in a strong, fake English accent. "And how is the Hernandez family enjoying the view?"

Sal delivered his answer in an equally strong, fake English accent. "Jolly good to be home soon, mate."

Kate burst out laughing. "You're getting silly. Please, no more fake accents."

"No one has had enough sleep."

"Maria is right. Let's stop at a motel and get some rest." Kate gave Ethan a warm steady gaze.

Ethan instantly raised both eyebrows. "What? Get a motel? We'll be at the farmhouse in less than eight hours."

"And probably have to clean it before we unpack."

"Oh." He glanced at his wife and seemed genuinely surprised. "You know what? It probably is dusty."

Sal nodded. "Motel time."

They continued staring out the windows as the road through town took them back onto the highway. Later, a floodlight illuminated a sign stating lodging for The Holiday Inn Express was ahead at the next exit.

"Holiday Inn Express sounds great. Does anyone know what town we are in?" Maria asked.

"Tulsa, Oklahoma. I saw the welcome sign." Ethan sounded tired.

They spotted the hotel near the exit ramp.

"Looks really nice to me." Kate pulled into the parking lot, and both men soon paid for one night's lodging. Kate hurriedly escorted Rufus to a fenced dog area before each family quietly went to their own room. No one mentioned eating. Weary, they slept for over eight hours. The following morning, they awoke hungrily.

The Holiday Inn Express offered a tremendous breakfast buffet. The steam tables smelled like a baker's oven. The aroma of fresh yeast rolls wafted through the air mixed with the strong scent of iced cinnamon rolls. The selection of sausage and turkey bacon fried in butter promised a savory taste to add to the meal. An abundance of fruit, as well as soft scrambled eggs in butter, omelets, and oatmeal cooked with the lingering scent of cinnamon and delectable chunks of apple, tempted your sense of smell and your tastebuds.

After several trips to the buffet tables, the famished group had their fill. They brushed breadcrumbs off their laps, and Maria wiped off warm cinnamon icing that had dribbled onto the chins of the children. Sticky fingers were next.

The adults quietly enjoyed another hot cup of coffee, and Ethan glanced at Kate.

"Would you call the electric company in Crockett, and make sure the power is on at the farmhouse? I know I talked to the water and gas companies, but I'm not sure if I called the electric company." He dug into his pocket and retrieved a scribbled phone number. Handing it to her, he made his way through incoming customers and veered toward the cashier.

"Sal, I'll take the kids to the restroom." Maria stood abruptly facing her husband.

She left with Carlos and Rosa, and Sal took another sip of his coffee.

Kate punched in the number for the electric company on her phone.

"Crockett Co-Op."

"Yes, I'm Kate Meyers. I'm calling to confirm the power has been turned on at 31924 Sun Valley Road."

"That's the old Meyers farmhouse, isn't it?"

"Yes ma'am."

"And you are?"

"I'm Kate Meyers, Ethan Meyers's wife."

"That can't be right. His wife died. I watched the investigation unfold on the national news."

"You are referring to his late wife, Becky Meyers."

"I'm sorry. I can't release any information about that account other than to Ethan Meyers. It's in his name, not your name. It's company policy."

"We simply want to know if the power is on."

"I'm sorry ma'am."

"But it's not like I'm changing the name on the account…"

The employee interrupted. "We couldn't let that happen without Mr. Meyers…"

Kate interrupted her. "I understand. I'll have Ethan call you himself. Sorry to have bothered you."

Kate ended the call and drew her mouth into a tight line. With nostrils flaring, she muttered under her breath as Ethan returned.

He glanced at her with a half-smile.

"Are you fuming? I've never seen my wife upset."

Kate tossed her hair about with disdain. "I'm trying to remain calm. The lady at the electric company treated me like I planned to hack your precious account."

Ethan lost his smile. His former tranquil face grew disturbed by a hard clenching of his jaw.

"I'm sorry she treated you rudely."

"It's okay. She merely followed company policy."

"So, is the power on at the farmhouse?"

"I don't know. She wouldn't tell me."

Sal leaned forward putting his elbows on the table. "Excuse me but I have to speak up. I understand an employee following company procedure, but what she did we refer to as being 'Large and In Charge.' She has the power to control, and she clearly enjoys it."

Ethan ran his fingers through his hair and snatched at the slip of paper. He punched the number in wrong and started over.

He sat in his chair holding the phone near Kate as it rang.

"Crockett Co-Op."

"Hello, this is Ethan Meyers. I need…"

"Hi, Ethan. It's Judy Harris. We went to school together. Of course, everyone knew me as Judy Henry then."

"Judy, it's been a long time. I never expected to talk to an old school chum."

"Well, that's how it is here, small town and all."

"I remember. Say, listen, could you tell me if the power is on out at the farmhouse? I had my wife call, and…"

Judy interrupted. "Now, Ethan; how am I to know she really is your wife?"

"Judy, I am married to Kate…"

"You have to fill out a new form if you want her on the account."

"Okay, I will. Mail it to me. Meanwhile, I want the electricity turned on at the farmhouse."

"It is on, Ethan. You called and talked to someone else a few days ago."

"I do remember now."

"I guess this means you'll be moving back here?"

"Yes. Yes, we are."

"Well then, welcome back, Ethan."

"Thanks, Judy."

She ended the call and Ethan continued sitting in his chair as his chest rose and fell heavily.

Kate shoved a glass of water at him and smiled.

"How far away from Topeka is this small town, Crockett?"

"About twenty miles." He drank the water in one gulp.

"And how close is the farmhouse to Crockett?"

"Oh, it's isolated."

Chapter Two

Sal took his turn driving. After leaving the main highway, he discovered spotty GPS accuracy. Ethan directed him through the maze of back roads, and Sal finally turned onto the private road of the Meyers estate.

Lowering the window flooded his senses with the fresh smell of adjoining hay fields. He slowed the vehicle. The crunch of gravel under the tires seemed to alert everyone to the end of their trip.

Excitement mounted as they spoke at once.

"Stop the car."

Sal parked on the side of the road, and Ethan left the car with a burst of energy.

"Come on! Experience this sunny day. No city fumes. Simply good ole' country air."

Wind feathered through the acres of uncut hay growing about four feet tall. The gentle swaying had a calming effect on the group as they exited the vehicle and stared mesmerized.

"A glimpse of heaven," Maria whispered. "I had no idea of the enormous peace and beauty here."

"Where are the cows?" Carlos tugged at his father's pants leg.

Sal glanced at Ethan with an expected look on his face.

"In other pastures, nearby," Ethan answered. "My neighbors raise grass-fed cattle, hundreds of them."

"And I'm sure they make delicious steaks." Sal speculated softly.

"Oh, yes."

"I can't wait." Kate strolled to Ethan and slipped her arm around his waist. "This is going to be like heaven for me too."

He bent over and planted a kiss on her forehead. "I'm glad. Hey, can I share our news with them?"

"Yes." She beamed.

He turned and faced Sal and Maria. "Kate and I want to adopt. We both love children and want our family to grow in numbers here at the farmhouse."

"Congratulations! And you two will make great parents. I think children running and playing and growing up is perfect for here."

"Thanks, so do we. Well, let's go. Let's see the rest of it."

The group climbed in the car, and Sal drove off with the window remaining down. He drove for several miles on a winding road until finally topping a hill. The flat land expanded as far as the eye could see. Straight ahead, in the far distance, you could distinguish a tiny farmhouse, surrounded by specks of something dark.

"We're here," Ethan shouted. Leaning forward facing the windshield, he scanned the horizon and frowned.

"What are the dots?" Sal glanced at Ethan. "Surely not..."

"Cows? I hope not."

Sal continued driving, and Ethan emitted a groan as the dots grew into cattle. Some had to be dodged as they maneuvered to remain on the road.

At the end of the gravel road stood the farmhouse, surrounded by a five-foot-tall metal fence with a thirty-foot-tall iron sign arched over the driveway. Spaced perfectly across the archway, the name 'MEYERS' hung at the exact location where the gravel road became a concrete driveway. Over a hundred cattle scattered across the well-manicured lawn, and the stench of sunbaked cow manure wafted into the car.

"I can't believe this." Kate moaned and wrinkled her nose.

Ethan snatched his phone and started punching numbers.

A few yards from the car, one cow proceeded through several piles of fresh manure. Flies buzzed as the animal plodded along. The foul order rose, and Kate gagged.

Sal closed his window.

"Who are you calling?"

"My neighbor."

Upon discussing the wandering cows, the neighbor assured Ethan he would take care of the situation and apologized.

Ethan had Sal drive as close to the front porch as possible, and they exited the car.

"Careful where you walk," Ethan called out his warning, but unfortunately not soon enough.

"Eeww!" Rosa gasped as she stepped into a brown, gooey mess.

Sal removed her shoe and left it on the ground. Everyone hurried up the steps and to the safety of the porch.

"At least they haven't trampled up here." Maria sighed as she glanced at the floor.

"Not yet. I don't think they've been out of their pasture long." Ethan unlocked the front door but didn't enter. He turned and plopped into one of many wooden, rocking chairs on the long porch. He sat facing the front lawn, eyes fixed on the driveway. Kate joined him.

Maria took the children to the old-fashioned porch swing. Sal paced the floor watching the cows graze the flower beds.

Thirty minutes later, the neighbor and a caravan of his employees arrived pulling long cattle trailers behind their trucks. The men and two dogs sprang from the trucks and hurried to round up the cattle. The short-legged dogs loped after the stray cows completely unafraid. Between the yapping of the dogs, and the whooping of the men; the cattle were soon manipulated into the trailers.

Ethan approached the older man who stood near his truck as the caravan left. Frowning, he continued examining the damaged lawn.

"Charles, it's been a while." Ethan extended his hand to his neighbor.

His weather-beaten face held eye contact with Ethan as they shook hands. "Yes, and a lot has changed since you've been gone."

"That goes for me as well."

"Sorry about your wife. No one wants to hear their spouse's death made the national news."

"Thank you. I didn't think I'd ever marry again, but God did. I am a firm believer He had me meet Kate when we did for that reason." Ethan nodded towards Kate. She gave Charles a shy smile, and Charles turned his full attention to her.

"Ma'am. It's a pleasure to meet you."

"And you also." Kate rose from the rocker, and she, Maria, and the children entered the house.

Sal eased off the porch and cautiously walked toward the two men.

"Ethan said you had grass-fed cattle, but this is beyond my imagination." He grinned.

Charles gave a slight smile and seemed preoccupied as he fidgeted with the brim of his hat. "No, it's not what you'd expect to find. Check this out." He motioned to Ethan and strolled towards the fence near the side of the house. Ethan followed as Sal brought up the rear.

"Looks like someone cut the fence wire."

All four strands of barbed wire lay on the ground between two sections of fence posts.

"Why would anyone do that? Charles, it's never happened before."

"Not to my knowledge."

"Some wire should still be in the barn, I'll…"

"No Ethan. I'm leasing your pasture. I'll fix it. I keep supplies on my truck."

They hastened to Charles's truck and Sal stopped.

"I don't know anything about repairing a fence. Ethan, I think I'll start unloading the car."

"Thanks. That'll be a big help."

Sal nodded and took several tote bags to the house.

Kate and Maria had left the children in the living room. Rosa placed her colors and a coloring book on the coffee table, and Carlos sat on the floor opening a box of Lego building blocks with a spaceship on the front. Sal smiled at his children and at first, he followed the women's subdued voices into the kitchen. Their angry discussion grew louder as he approached.

He noticed Kates's face etched with worry. Glancing at his wife, he saw the deep frown creasing her forehead. Sal then caught a twinkle of sunlight on something in the room and suddenly starred in amazement. He scanned the room in silence as slivers of glass covered the countertops, and everything in the room. The table, chairs, stove, and floor all glistened in the rays of sunlight pouring in from the busted windows. Particles of glass glittered in the curtains as a light breeze sailed in.

He spotted the large rocks lying on the floor. Some were the size of a grapefruit, and one had a note attached to it by a rubber band.

"Don't touch it." Maria's voice trailed off.

"I've called 9-1-1. The dispatcher is sending deputies." Kate swung her arm through the air. "We aren't cleaning any of this until they see it."

Sal ran outside yelling. "Ethan, hurry, come into the kitchen."

Ethan glanced at Charles and both men dropped the barbed wire and sprinted to the house. Ethan then rushed past Charles and Sal and made his way to the kitchen.

Looking straight at Kate, and out of breath, he held onto the frame of the doorway. "What?"

Kate pointed to the large rocks on the floor, and he instantly saw the shattered glass.

His face paled as he entered the room and walked toward one of the rocks.

"No. Don't. Sheriff deputies are on the way."

A siren screamed in the distance and Ethan froze.

Chapter Three

The sirens screamed unbearably loud; piercing eardrums at close range when the noise abruptly stopped as if an agonizing animal were suddenly put out of its misery right on the front lawn. Two doors slammed outside breaking Ethan's mesmerized state. After an involuntary shudder, he darted through the house exiting on the porch.

"Gentlemen, I'm sure glad to see you."

Both deputies nodded. Cautiously, they side-stepped countless fresh piles of manure until finally standing on the raised front porch. Scanning the splattered area, they turned to Ethan.

"This must be the problem. Nasty mess."

"Part of it." Ethan extended his hand to the nearest deputy. "Ethan Meyers, I'm the homeowner."

"Ira Pascal and this is my partner, Caleb Davis. What happened here?"

"Mischief. Barbed wire has been cut on the side fence, and my neighbor's cattle ruined the lawn. Rocks were thrown into the kitchen busting out windows. Shattered glass is all over. It's a disaster."

The deputy nodded at Ethan. "Where is the kitchen located?"

"At the back of the house."

"Stay here. We'll check it out."

Off in a hurry, the deputies' brisk walk soon paused. Approaching the corner of the house, a campsite loomed against the back wall. Weapons drawn; they secured the area. The makeshift tent held cans of food, and bottled water. A nearby circle of rocks formed a much-used campfire. Blankets and trash littered the yard. Deputy Pascal squatted and felt the dirt in the campfire.

"Still warm."

Both deputies squinted scanning surrounding pastures for signs of movement, but only the occasional lonesome calling of a whippoorwill broke the eerie stillness. Deputy Davis took pictures from various angles, and they strolled back to the front of the house.

"Mr. Meyers, has anyone been bothering you lately?"

"Why, no. No one. We returned to the property today, moving in to stay. I haven't lived here in years. It's been vacant since my mother passed away."

"Anyone know you are moving back?"

"No, but I did contact the utility companies to resume service."

Deputy Pascal instantly smiled at Ethan. "Talk to Judy Harris?"

Ethan's brow furrowed into a deep frown. "Yes."

"Then the whole town knows you're back. Anyone here who might object to your return?"

"Not that I'm aware of. Never had an enemy if that's what you are suggesting."

"Well, that's good to know, because whoever is camping out in your backyard, definitely doesn't want you here."

"Camping out?" Ethan spit the words out in a loud rage.

"Camping out. We'll keep an eye on it. Hopefully catch the perpetrator, or perpetrators soon. You can look at the campsite but leave it alone. We'll need to take pictures of the damage in the kitchen. After that, you and your family must leave. You can stay at a local motel, but I wouldn't talk about this to anyone. Your home is now a crime scene."

Charles shook his head. "Ethan, if I can help in any way, let me know. I'll go now, and don't hesitate to call."

Ethan nodded at his old friend. "I appreciate that." He watched as Charles started the truck and drove away.

He and the weary travelers steered toward the back of the house and observed the campsite in silence.

Maria kept the children close to her as soon as she saw the scattered debris and makeshift tent of filthy blankets.

"Shocking," Sal muttered under his breath. "How is this possible?" He glanced at Ethan.

"Especially out here." Ethan shook his head as they viewed the clutter and trash. Kate quietly sidestepped a pile of clothing and ducked her head peering into the tent.

"Don't touch anything..." Everyone spoke to her at once.

"I'm not." She tilted her head and leaned forward. "Oh, my goodness... is it? Yes, it is...lots of empty cans of peaches, Vienna sausage, crackers, cans of tuna, and...oh, no...empty boxes of baby wipes and toddler pull-ups..." Her voice broke with emotion.

She inched closer and appeared to consider the contents inside the tent when Ethan tugged at her arm.

"Come on, we need to get out of here." He gently escorted her to the front of the house while the others followed.

"I'm sorry I got so close to the tent, but I simply can't stand the idea of a baby being in that dirty place." Kate sputtered.

"I agree. It's hard to comprehend."

Kate, Maria, and the children resumed their seats in the car as Sal and Ethan returned from the house with personal belongings needed for overnight.

Deputy Pascal waited for Ethan on the porch. "Mr. Meyers, you could be at the motel for several days. We'll need to call you about any developments."

They exchanged contact information. Ethan locked the house and turned to leave.

"Mr. Meyers, I'll need that key. We'll have someone inside waiting for the campers to return and have remote outside observation by drones."

"Really? So, drones will fly around with cameras?"

"Makes surveillance a whole lot easier."

Ethan nodded and walked to the Chevy. He ran his hands through his hair and looked at Sal. "We're not leaving the farmhouse; we're leaving a crime scene."

"It's crazy." Sal gazed at the farmhouse again, and they slowly left.

Conversation dwindled inside the car. It appeared everyone's energy level had been zapped by the encounter. Shoulders soon slumped, as silence took over.

Vacancies were available at the motel outside of town. Settling in their rooms, and later quietly eating at the nearby restaurant did have a sense of normalcy about it. Watching the children in the motel's play area also seemed to settle everyone's nerves.

"Please, don't discuss the farmhouse in front of Carlos or Rosa. They'll have nightmares tonight." Maria glanced at the group of adults, and everyone nodded.

Finally, goodnights were said as they returned to their rooms for the night. Ethan took Rufus outside and they soon ambled back to the room.

All appeared calm with the worst behind them. All except for Kate.

***

My mind cranked out countless worse-case scenarios, and I realized I heard pounding in my ears.

Is this giving me high blood pressure?...

My heart continued to race and pound as I considered the recent turmoil of this morning.

Who is the enemy, and why?

"Kate? Kate, let's go back to bed." Ethan's voice emitted a calmness I could feel as his obvious concern swept over me.

"Oh, Ethan, I didn't want to wake you."

He leaned over my chair and smiled.

One slow stroke of his hand across the curly mop of hair on my head, and my tension eased.

I glanced at him and squeezed his hand.

"Thanks."

"Tough days are faced like the good ones. Remember, we are in this together."

"I know, and I'm trying not to worry. I …uh…I can't shake this bad feeling I have about the whole situation."

"Kate, both deputies assured us they will find the culprit, and they will. They took pictures and obtained plenty of evidence. Give them time to do their job. Our losing sleep over this won't help anything. Stress isn't good either."

"But the rock…the note," I muttered as he took my arm and eased me from the chair in front of the picture window.

"Kate, 'Get out now' written on a note does not mean I'm going back to Houston. I'm only leaving temporarily until this is legally solved. This is my home, and the authorities will help stop this invasion."

One final stare out the window as moonlight peeped through the trees across the parking lot. Dotted with a few vehicles, it seemed unbelievable to even be here. I followed Ethan to the king-size bed when he seized my hand.

"Let's pray for peace."

I felt relieved and nodded at my husband as he led us in prayer.

Chapter Four

Holding baby Elsa on my hip, I waded through the creek with muddy water squishing inside my torn tennis shoes. At twenty-four months old, holding her had become a struggle. She wiggled and wanted to play. A strong breeze lifted my hair and twirled under my shirt as a foul order engulfed me. Realization slowly came as I gasped, and I knew the smell emitted from my own body.

Gina girl, you may be free, but your smell will get you caught…

Wrinkling my nose, joy still filled my mind. I managed to escape the creepy guy, Douglas.

Numb from scrapes off of tree

branches, I plodded on smell and all. Elsa laughed as I tripped on a root protruding from the creek bed.

Have to be more careful.

I miss the campsite Elsa and I had behind an empty house. No great living conditions there, but safe? Yes. Safe that is until the guy named Douglas snooped around and caught us. He arrived without any food, and his sneakiness frightened me. Mean and filthy, he thought I should be submissive to him. I may be in a bad situation, but no one is going to be in control of me or my baby, not in my camp or anywhere else. Leaving him in the middle of the night had been such a relief. Hard to believe I left two weeks ago, and he still hasn't found me. He may not be looking for me, though. I hope he's not.

I have to get help and I have to get a job.

Glancing at Elsa, I knew we could do it. Finding a babysitter still gnawed at me, but I'd figure it out. My oversized shoulder purse bulged with food and supplies, and I'd be fine without Douglas. I didn't like the way he yelled at Elsa anyway.

Chapter Five

Ethan lay on his back; hands folded behind his head and replayed the day's events over and over in his mind. Someone invading his property bothered him deeply. He didn't want to worry Kate, but it did consume him.

Looking at her sleeping peacefully, he carefully left the bed, got his Bible off the side end table, and eased into the chair by the front window.

God, I need Your help. I need Your guidance.

He opened his Bible and flipped through the pages stopping to read the book of II Timothy. When he came to chapter 3, he reread verses one through six out loud.

II Timothy 3:1-6

1: This know also, that in the last days perilous times shall come. 2: For men shall be lovers of their own selves, covetous, boasters, proud, blasphemers, disobedient to parents, unthankful, unholy, 3: Without natural affection, trucebreakers, false accusers, incontinent, fierce, despisers of those who are good. 4: Traitors, heady, high-minded, lovers of pleasures more than lovers of God. 5: Having a form of Godliness, but denying the power thereof: from such turn away. 6: For of this sort are they which creep into houses, and lead captive silly women laden with sins, led away with divers lusts.

He continued reading and with his yellow highlighter, marked each verse in chapters 3 and 4.

Talking to himself, he mumbled out loud, "I think verse six in chapter 3 refers to ways of false teaching and how women would fall for a false preacher before a man would as women could fall for the lust of the false preacher who would be a man…"

"I can see how that could happen." Kate sat upright in the bed.

"Oh, I'm sorry, Kate. Did I wake you?"

"No, I'm dozing off and on."

He rubbed his eyes and yawned.

"I couldn't sleep. Decided to get some direction and ended up reading II Timothy."

"Good for you. One of my favorite scriptures comes to mind and I think it pertains to our situation. Psalms 55:22 Cast your burdens upon the LORD, and He shall sustain you: He shall never suffer the righteous to be moved."

"We need to pray again. Let's do it."

They bowed their heads and Ethan led them in prayer. "Heavenly Father, we can't handle this situation alone. You can do so much more with it than we ever could. We turn all our burdens over to You, and we do not want them back. We trust You to fight our battles for us and we have our trust and faith in You according to Your Word. Forgive us of our sins and we won't repeat them, and we forgive our enemies and pray they come to know You as their Savior. In Jesus' name we pray, Amen."

"Amen," Kate added.

Ethan's phone played its doorbell ring alerting him of a received text message, and they both looked at each other startled.

"What time is it?"

"A quarter to midnight."

Ethan snatched his smartphone off the dresser and glanced at the message.

"Well, the deputy said he'd call if there were any new developments. Looks like they spotted a fire at the campsite. Someone did cook on the campfire but left."

Kate yawned. "I really didn't believe anyone would be caught because they'd be too stupid to return. Or even too bold to return so quickly, don't you think?"

"Yes, and I'm beginning to feel we won't be safe as long as he or she or they remain free."

"We turned it over to the Lord, remember?"

"Thanks for reminding me. God's got this."

"No more doubt." She nodded and scooted under the comforter and fluffed her pillow.

"Kate, are you still glad we came to Kansas? I mean what with this happening and how rude Judy Harris treated you?"

"Of course, I'm still glad we are here. You have no control over other people. No one does. You never know what someone else might say or do…"

Ethan interrupted her. "Or what their ulterior motive is."

"Exactly. It all goes back to the devil who comes to steal, kill, and destroy. But we wear the full armor of God and have His Word for protection. And we've got it."

Ethan stepped lightly to the bed and as she rolled over with her back to him, he threw his pillow at her.

"Yes, ma'am." He laughed and turned out the light.

"Wait for paybacks." Kate proceeded to wad her pillow into a ball as Ethan flipped the light back on.

Her pillow sailed across the bed and missed Ethan as they both gazed at each other with a sly smile.

"Goodnight, Ethan."

He returned the pillow to her, grinned, and turned out the light again.

"Goodnight, Kate."

Ethan tossed and turned until

the early morning hours. It did not disturb Kate, though, and she softly snored. Feeling hot and clammy, he finally kicked his side of the covers to the foot of the bed. Amazed to be sweating, he silently trekked in the dark to the overnight bag on the dresser searching for extra strength Tylenol to break the fever. A bottle of Listerine mouthwash fell out and hit the floor bouncing.

"What?" Kate mumbled and turned on the lamp at her side of the bed.

"Do we have Tylenol?"

"No, I forgot to bring it. Why?"

"I have a fever and my stomach

is starting to feel queasy."

"Oh, Ethan, I hate that. Maybe it's something you ate."

"I'm getting acid indigestion now. I guess the baked fish I had earlier is the culprit."

"The rest of us had spaghetti. Did your fish taste too fishy? Did it smell bad?"

"I don't know. Baked fish tastes fishy. I don't always savor every bite. I eat it because it's healthy." Slipping on his sweatpants and sweatshirt, he shifted his stance toward Kate. "I'm going to that all-night store we passed on the way here; I'll be right back."

"Wait, I'll go with you." Kate struggled with the wadded-up cover and tried to sit upright.

"No, it won't take long. Go to sleep." He grabbed his billfold and keys and bent to lightly kiss her. "I'll only be gone a few minutes."

"Well, all right." She drew the covers close and rolled over.

Ethan dismissed the wave of dizziness that overcame him as he drove out of the motel parking lot. The intensity came and went as he approached the store. Upon arrival though, as he exited his vehicle, he trembled with a sudden weakness in his legs. He continued on, entering the store as he stumbled, steadying himself by holding onto a rack of potato chips.

Chapter Six

Kurt, standing behind the counter filling the candy display, heard the loud thud as a man fell to the floor. His twin brother, Karl heard it too and came running from aisle four where he had been stocking shelves. The stranger lay motionless as a small pool of blood grew on the floor surrounding his head. Karl yanked his phone from his pants pocket and dialed 911.

"This is Karl Schuhmacher at Jarmann Market. Send an ambulance quickly. Some man is laying on the floor and isn't moving."

"Jarmann Market? What is the

address, sir?"

"Corner of Richmond Road and Baltasar."

"Does he have a pulse?"

Karl didn't hesitate to push his forefinger against the man's neck.

"Yes, ma'am, but his head is bleeding where it hit the floor."

"We have an ambulance and a deputy on the way."

A patrol car soon stopped directly at the front door of the store, leaving its lights flashing as the deputy rushed inside.

He bent over the injured man and felt a faint pulse.

"Sir, sir can you hear me?"

Upon not receiving an answer, the deputy reached into the man's pocket for his billfold. He frowned as he scrutinized the driver's license information.

"Houston? This guy is from Houston? What's he doing up here in Kansas?" He studied the license again. "His name is Ethan Meyers. Do either of you know him?"

"No sir, but I've heard the name. Our neighbor Judy talked about him yesterday." Karl scratched his head. "Small world."

"Small world indeed."

EMS arrived and began taking Ethan's vital signs.

The deputy pivoted to the two employees. "What are your names?"

"I'm Karl Schuhmacher, and this is my brother Kurt."

"Well, one of you get this Judy on the phone. Maybe she can give me some information on Mr. Meyers. He's certainly not able to."

Kurt phoned her immediately.

"Ms. Judy, someone needs to talk to you, and here he is." Kurt handed his phone to the deputy.

"Who is this?" Judy demanded.

"Ma'am, sorry to disturb you, this is Deputy Foley, and we have a man who is unconscious. His name is Ethan Meyers, and I need any information you may have pertaining to him."

"Oh yes, I know him. You say

he's unconscious? Maybe this new woman did him in, I don't know. I don't know her, she's not from here. I went to school with him in our younger years. Ethan recently moved back from Houston. Now, I don't go for gossip, but you need to know about the rumor… he supposedly killed his wife there…"

Deputy Foley interrupted. "Ma'am, excuse me but…"

Judy continued. "The news described Ethan as a person of interest, and then they found her body. I know he does have a new woman with him now, but I don't know for how long…"

"Ma'am…I think I have enough information…"

"He tried to say they were married when I talked to him the other day."

"You talked to him?"

"Yes, he had the electricity turned on at his house."

"Can you recall the address by any chance?"

"Yes, it's at his old home place. He used to live there. It's 31924 Sun Valley Road."

"Thank you, ma'am, you've helped tremendously."

EMS workers had Ethan on a stretcher and were placing him into the ambulance.

Deputy Foley handed the phone back to Kurt. "Thank you, young man."

He hastened to his patrol car and glanced at the paramedic. "I'll lead you to the hospital."

As fast as the situation happened, it abruptly ended. Kurt and Karl watched as both vehicles left in an urgency seen only by them.

"Lord help him," Karl muttered.

"Amen," Kurt added.

Red and blue lights flashed silently as the car and ambulance hurried out of sight. No customers were there. Not many people out at three o'clock in the morning, though.

Chapter Seven

Kate rolled over in bed. Her arm slid across to Ethan's pillow and down his side of the bed.

Still gone? What time is it?

Pitching the covers to the floor, she felt her way in the darkness to her phone on the dresser. The time on the phone read 3:15 AM. Icy chills instantly rushed over her. Shivering, worse-case scenarios flooded her mind.

No, he can't be gone that long…maybe I looked at the time wrong…

A darting glance at the phone confirmed the time.

Definitely 3:15 AM…

Kate hurried to change clothes and ran outside barely closing the door. Racing down the sidewalk to find Sal and Maria, she frantically located room number 305. Pounding on their door, she yelled in a high pitch tone. "Sal, Maria, it's me, Kate. Please let me in." Her loud demands quickly turned into cries of anguish.

Maria jerked the door open, and Kate rushed forward hugging her former neighbor. "Ethan got sick. He's been gone… to the…the store…" She sobbed harder and could no longer talk.

"We'll find him. It's okay." Maria rubbed Kate across her shoulders until Kate's body no longer shook with each breath. The hard sobbing ceased, and Kate looked at Maria with red-rimmed eyes. "He went to get Tylenol and should have been back a long time ago. He told me to go back to sleep. Oh, I'm afraid something bad has happened to him."

Sal exited the bathroom fully dressed in jeans, a pullover top, and sneakers. The children's frightened whimpering finally registered with Sal as he tried to approach Kate. Both Rosa and Carlos clung to his legs looking up at him wide-eyed. "Don't be afraid, it's only Kate." They loosened their grip and boldly stared at Kate.

"What store?"

"The all-night one we passed coming here."

"Go back to your room, Kate, and wait there in case he returns. I'll walk to the store and call you if I find anything."

"Okay, thanks." She tried in vain to wipe the tears streaming down her face and scampered off as Sal addressed his family.

"Pray for Ethan and Kate. I will pray as I go."

"Yes, and be careful, Sal. Call me."

He nodded at Maria, kissed her bye, and hurried outside. Always alert, he took in his surroundings and scanned the area before leaving. Nothing looked suspicious. One could never be too cautious in any environment though, at least that's what he learned watching true crime shows on television. Thankful for not seeing anyone else out and about; he sprinted a few blocks and prayed silently for his friends.

Relief filled his entire being when he spotted Ethan's Suburban parked at the side of the store's entrance. He displayed a relaxed appearance walking in. Kurt and Karl were still on edge, and both jumped at the sound of the bell clanging when Sal opened the front door. They watched him stroll by the end of several aisles obviously looking for someone.

"Can we help you?" Kurt leaned over the counter on his elbows.

"Yes, I saw my friend's car outside. I'm trying to find him." Sal approached the counter.

"What's your friend's name?"

"Ethan Meyers."

Kurt made eye contact with his brother and Karl nodded.

"Well, I'm sorry to tell you but he passed out in here, and the ambulance took him to the hospital."

Sal let out a low moan. "Oh, no…"

"He hit his head on the floor and lost consciousness."

"Thanks." Sal bolted out the door and called Kate.

"Get ready to go. Ethan's in the hospital. I'm on my way. We'll get an Uber ride." He hung up while his feet pounded the pavement. Finally, near the motel, he had to slow his speed. His lungs felt like they would burst. He couldn't catch his breath. He stopped and bent over, taking in short gulps of air. Kate came running to him from the motel parking lot. She had called the Uber ride and within minutes it arrived. A silent trip to the hospital and Sal paid the driver with his credit card. He and Kate grimaced at each other as they entered the hospital.

Kate ran straight to the admitting desk inside.

"I'm looking for my husband, Ethan Meyers. An ambulance brought him in a short time ago. Can you tell me where he is or how he is?"

"One moment, Ma'am."

The attendant buzzed someone. Kate absentmindedly tapped her fingernails on the desk and noticed several people in the waiting room. An elderly couple gazed at a newspaper. A young woman played peek-a-boo with an energetic toddler. One older man sprawled across a love seat snoring loudly oblivious of everyone. Another sat upright texting furiously on his smartphone. Kate frowned at Sal.

"My world is crashing apart, and others act like nothing's going on..." Her voice ended in a strained, high pitch.

"Kate, calm down. They can't possibly know you are worried about Ethan. They can't even know Ethan." Sal gushed.

"You're right. It seems surreal, though." The abrupt sound of loud footsteps caught Kate by surprise. Her whole body instantly jerked, and her hands fluttered in the air. Sal sucked in a quick breath. "Kate, please..."

"I'm sorry. I will try to be calm."

A police officer had entered the room from an adjoining hallway. His noisy approach over the tiled floor echoed like a faulty loudspeaker. It continued until finally stopping directly in front of Kate. He addressed her in a firm tone.

"May I help you?"

Kate fidgeted with her purse. "Yes, I'm trying to find out about my husband's condition. Ethan Meyers. An ambulance recently brought him here."

"I'm sorry, ma'am. We have reason to believe he is not married. You cannot see him, and by law, we cannot discuss anything with you."

"What are you talking about?" Kate screamed. "He is my husband. I demand to see him."

"I'm sorry, but we have reason to believe his life is in danger. He is in our protective custody."

"Life in danger? Protective custody? This is ludicrous." Kate glared at the officer, her chest rising and falling as air shot out of her nostrils.

"There has to be a mistake, officer. I know this couple, and I know they are married." Sal spoke as assuringly as possible under the circumstances.

Before the officer could reply, the attendant focused on Kate. "Ma'am bring a copy of your marriage license and you can see him. That's all we can do to help you."

"Let's go." Sal touched Kate's arm and discovered she was trembling. He walked her quickly to the exit doors and left the hospital. As the automatic doors were closing, a booming voice on the intercom blared for Dr. Spencer to come immediately to the O.R.

Kate immediately stopped on the sidewalk. "Did you hear that? I think they are doing something to Ethan."

"We can't go in there. Call an Uber, and then we'll call Houston for your marriage license."

Further down the hall inside an examining room, Ethan regained consciousness for a brief moment.

"Mr. Meyers? You've had a heart attack. We need your permission to operate. You have several blockages."

"Yes, yes, of course."

"We're going to give you something to make you sleep. Your eyelids will get heavy in a minute."

"Wait…my wife…my wife…" His voice trailed off as the medication took effect.

The local nurse shook her head at the doctor who administered the anesthesia.

"Poor man, he thinks his wife is still alive…"

Chapter Eight

"Judy?" The deep male voice sent shivers down her spine, and she remembered it immediately.

Could it be…after all this time…?

"Yes."

"It's me, Douglas. Douglas Futrell." His words seemed to hang in the air waiting on her response.

"I heard you are a Futrell now, and I also heard you were in prison."

"You heard right, but I'm legally out now. I'd like to see you."

Judy pushed some fallen curls

off her forehead with a shaky hand. "I'd like to see you too. I've moved now. I live in the old Ferguson home…"

He interrupted her. "I've kept up with local happenings. I know where you are."

"Well then…I'll see you soon."

His boisterous laughter caught her off guard. And her sudden frown wouldn't have been acceptable by him.

"I'll warn you, Judy, you might not recognize me. I have long hair and a full beard."

"Where in the world have you been with all the hair?"

"Camping. Hey, I have a plan that might benefit both of us. I'll tell you about it when I get there."

"You sly dog."

His laughter continued bellowing out as he ended the call.

Judy hurried to comb her hair and freshen her make-up. She lit a candle named Clementine Sunrise. A blend of clementine oranges, grapefruit, and citrus; the scent wafted across the living room calming her anxiety and settling her scattered thoughts, but her mind soon flooded with memories of Douglas.

He will not take control this time…he has such a demanding presence about him though…

She paused at the hallway

mirror catching a quick glimpse of her reflection. She tugged at a loose strand of hair across her cheekbone and shoved it behind her ear.

That'll have to do…I never thought of him as a boyfriend anyway…

The abrupt firm knock at the door startled her.

Hmm, he didn't pound on it. Maybe he has changed…no, not being in prison…not him.

She yanked the door open and gazed at the mass of unkempt hair on the filthy man. Dirty ribbons of dried sweat ran down his cheeks and grimy smudges were scattered about his face, neck, and arms. The thick beard fell over his chest rising with each breath he took. Judy parted her lips to speak, but the foul odor of Douglas seemed to hit her in her mouth. She choked.

His laughter filled the room as he pushed her aside and entered.

"I tried to warn you."

Judy closed the front door and followed him into the foyer.

"I'll need a bath. Where's your bathroom?"

"At the end of the hallway and take your time." He sauntered toward it and Judy stopped him.

"Wait. Let me get you a robe from my room." She darted off and returned with one.

"I'll throw my dirty clothes out later and you can run them through the washer and dryer." He snatched the robe and went into the bathroom. As the noisy water rushed full force in the bathtub, he yelled, "Hey, how are you at cutting hair?"

"I'm handy."

"Well, Ms. Handy, you can come and get my dirty clothes now. I may need two baths. Oh, and thanks."

Judy immediately retrieved the clothes and ran to the laundry room selecting a heavy wash cycle with two rinses on the washing machine. She listened as Douglas turned the blast of water off in the bathroom and went to the kitchen for scissors. She grabbed two from a drawer and with a deep sigh, she slumped into the nearest chair.

Chapter Nine

The police officer on duty had strolled several feet behind Kate and Sal as they left the hospital's entrance. Kate, listening to the blaring intercom, remained unaware of his presence, or that Sal had turned around and noticed him. She did, however, call for an Uber ride as Sal suggested, and it arrived in record time. The minute they slid into the back seat of the vehicle, the police officer spun on his heels and returned to working security inside the hospital.

"Where to?" The driver asked.

"Jarmann Market," Sal answered.

"I know where that is. It won't take long."

Kate absentmindedly rummaged through her purse and paused upon discovering the extra set of car keys Ethan had given her months ago. Not able to hide her happiness, she leaned toward the front window and watched as they passed various buildings with a smile that slowly grew from ear to ear. Sal narrowed his eyes at her as he watched the smile form across her face.

Barely audible, Kate mouthed the word 'car' as she dangled the keys at Sal.

"His car may not be there. They may have impounded it." Sal

whispered. "And you don't need to get in trouble."

"I don't think they've had time to discover it's his. He did park it on the side of the store."

"Well, you really are his wife. Half of that car is yours. They'll soon find out anyway." Sal shrugged.

"Whoop," she yelled as they approached the market, and Ethan's car came into view.

Kate beamed and paid the driver. As he drove off, her smile faded, and while walking, she prayed for Ethan's healing and comfort. She and Sal, alone in the parking lot, wearily made their way to the Chevy Suburban. She stood still for a moment at the car and stretched her arms in the air. Fatigue had set in on both of them. She reached to unlock the car and dropped the keys. Sal noticed her tired, red-rimmed eyes when she bent to retrieve them. At first, he hesitated but suddenly blurted in a strained tone, "Kate, I'll drive this time. Hand me the keys."

She started to speak but her voice trailed off. "I...uh..." Blinking at him, she handed over the keys and sank into the passenger's seat. Sal slipped behind the steering wheel, and they left.

"Let's find someplace to get coffee. We need to talk."

Kate nodded and rubbed the back of her neck as he drove along the main road in town. Minutes later, the golden arches of a local McDonald's loomed high on the horizon a few blocks away. Sal pulled into the half-full parking lot and exchanged a glance with Kate.

"Can you believe how busy they are at this hour of the morning?"

She shook her head. With a stooped posture, she leaned toward the car door, opening it the instant he parked. Sal observed the now rumpled clothing she'd obviously thrown on earlier. Taking her inside, he selected a table without customers nearby. He left her there and returned with two steaming cups of coffee.

"Kate, I know you are tired, but we need a plan. I've been silently praying about all of this."

"So have I. Whatever we do must be God's will, or it won't work."

"I agree."

Kate turned her head and gazed around the room, never settling on a person or object for long.

Two older men entered heading straight to the counter. Chatter from others drowned out their order and Kate jumped as Sal spoke in a friendly tone.

"Hey, can I have your attention?" Sal's slight smile displayed kindness that Kate couldn't ignore.

"Sorry, my mind is racing."

"We are both tired and Ethan would want us to keep trying." He sipped his coffee and fell silent as the two men brought their food trays to the table behind Kate.

"I won't ever stop trying, Sal, and I thank you for helping, especially being as weary as we are. I might contact Pastor Williford in Houston. He has contacts there who can speed the process of obtaining my marriage certificate."

"If anyone can, he is our answer."

Kate reached for her drink as one of the two men at the next table stumbled and fell landing on the floor against her chair. Coffee spilled dripping off her table. The man lost his grasp on the two empty metal food trays, and the noise as they clattered to the floor stopped all conversation.

Sal leaped to his feet and helped the man stand.

"Are you okay?" Sal asked.

"Yes, embarrassed though. Guess I needed more rest before making this trip." He grinned and retrieved the trays.

"Here, I'll take those." His friend grabbed the trays and nodded at Kate and Sal as the men went to the awaiting food at their table.

An employee arrived, cleaned the area, and soon brought Kate another cup of coffee.

"Back to our discussion." Sal continued. "We can't stay at the farmhouse and living at the motel is not an option. I need to find work, and I need to find it fast. I know you, and you'll be at that hospital daily until they let you visit Ethan."

"And I know they won't let me see him, but maybe someone working there can give me an update on his condition."

"I'm not sure, Kate. Maybe. But I will ask around town if anyone is hiring. I may be new here, but I do have references they can check out."

"I could try, too…" Her voice trailed off.

"Kate, you couldn't focus on anything except your husband in the hospital. It's possible my wife and I might both get a job, and you'd babysit the kids for us. That would be nice." He downed the last of his coffee and stood to leave.

"Wait while I go to the restroom." Kate took off, and Sal settled back into his chair.

"Young man."

Sal looked around as the man at the next table turned to face him.

"Excuse me. I couldn't help overhearing you needing a job. I'm Hubert Chisum." He extended his hand to Sal who promptly shook it.

"Sal Hernandez, and yes sir, I do need a job."

"And this is my brother, Monroe."

"Ever work on a farm?" Hubert leaned forward and narrowed his eyes at Sal before Sal could acknowledge Monroe.

"No sir, but I can learn."

"Any references?"

"Yes, sir, in Houston. Comet Auto Supply bought out Brock's Auto. I managed both for over twenty years, not at the same time of course. I had to leave because of Hurricane Harvey. Recently relocated here with my wife and two children and my neighbors."

Monroe raised his eyebrows at his brother. Hubert nodded.

"I'll need at least five people I can call, and I will check you out thoroughly. Have you been in jail?"

"No sir."

"Do drugs?"

"No sir."

Monroe rubbed his chin with his hand. "Tell me, do you ever go to church?"

"We are Baptists. Left a great church family."

"Write the names down and phone numbers if you have them." Monroe gave him a small notebook from his pocket and a pen.

Sal began writing as Kate returned. Her steps halted as she spotted the two men hovering over him as he sat at the table writing.

"Sal?" Kate spoke quietly.

He glanced at her, and his face beamed. "Kate, I'm applying for a job."

"Oh, thank you, Lord Jesus!" She grinned at the men and regained her confidence. "He is a good man; one you can rely on. I do hope you consider him for whatever the job is. I'm Kate Meyers. Sal and his family are our neighbors from Houston."

"Nice to meet you, ma'am. I'm Hubert Chisum and this is my brother Monroe."

They exchanged brief smiles.

Sal completed the information and handed the notebook and pen back to Monroe. After glancing at it, Monroe handed it to Hubert.

"Looks good to me. Might as well check it out now." Hubert

grabbed the smartphone from his pocket, and Sal watched as he punched in an email address. Within minutes, Sal saw the report with his name on it.

Hubert and Monroe both took their time reading it.

Sal tried to look at something else…anything…in the restaurant to keep his eyes off the report, and Kate, now seated, squirmed in her chair.

"I thought this would take days to check into my background," Sal whispered to Kate.

Hubert's voice boomed as he interrupted Sal. "Young man, the jobs and names you listed were on this report." He made eye contact with Sal. "And it's one of the best reports I've seen. You passed." He shook Sal's hand again. "I think you'll like the job. You'll take over the business my entrepreneur sister had started. Process orders, mail the product, do inventory, bookkeeping, the whole shebang. She has Alzheimer's now. That business meant a lot to her, and I want to try and keep it going as long as I can. I have a caretaker's house you and your family can live in for free. You'll work forty hours a week at $18.00 an hour and off weekends."

"I'll take it, but could Kate stay with us? Her husband is in the hospital and…"

"Of course."

"Thank you, sir."

"Don't you want to know what the product you'll be working with is?"

"I don't care. I'm happy to get the job, and I'll do my best to keep the business going."

"Good. I have to drive to Kansas City this morning. Monroe will get you settled in and show you everything."

He stood, first nodding at Kate, then Sal and Monroe, and left. He appeared zapped of energy as they watched him walk out the door. His posture slumped, and his face flushed slightly when he turned and waved at them.

Monroe spoke in a gentle tone. "He'll be back in a week. Hopefully, he won't have to drive there again."

Sal and Kate looked questioningly at each other and remained silent.

"Well, let me draw you a map to our place. You can get started moving in."

He withdrew the same notebook from his shirt pocket and carefully named roads as he wrote them on the paper. "I added the zip code in case you want to use the GPS. I don't care for it myself; it distracts me while I'm driving."

Kate nodded and shot Sal a hopeful glance. "Maybe we could drive out to Ethan's farmhouse and get the trailer with all of our belongings."

"Great idea. We'll get Maria and the kids first from the motel, then swing over to get the trailer. Can you get over this? It's a miracle! God has his hand on us, Kate."

"Yes, he does. And we'll continue praying for healing and comfort for Ethan." She watched as Monroe completed the map and handed it to Sal.

"I put my phone number there also, in case you get lost. Call me either way so I'll know when to expect you."

"Will do. And thank you again sir."

Monroe left, and Kate and Sal both whooped out loud with excitement.

"Come on, let's get started. I don't know about you, but that has revived me." Sal's eyes danced with merriment and Kate couldn't stop smiling.

"Me too."

Neither talked as he drove to the motel to get Maria, Carlos, and Rosa. He soon whistled as they drove into the parking lot.

Sal unlocked the door while calling out to his wife. Maria stumbled into his arms as he entered the room.

"I've been so worried." Her chin trembled as she spoke.

"It's okay. Everything is okay." Sal caressed her cheek, and she gave him a slight smile.

Kate walked closer to Maria and patted her shoulder.

"We should have called you, but things happened so fast. Sal is right, everything is okay now. In fact, this turned out to be a good day."

"Ethan is being cared for in the hospital, and I have a new job, and…" he paused and grinned at Maria.

"And? And tell me!" She demanded.

"And all of us have a place to live where I'll be working."

Maria burst into Spanish before she realized it. "Cuántas bendiciones temenos!"

"Yes, Maria." He laughed and hugged her. "We have many blessings."

"I agree," Kate added. "But it almost seems too good to be true. Wait a minute." Her voice quivered as nervousness took over. "We need to slow down. This may really be too good to be true …let's check them out. It works both ways. We need to know all about them before we move out there."

"We don't know their friends or their work history." Maria blurted.

"Small town, Maria. Everybody knows everybody." Sal glanced at his wristwatch. "In five more minutes, it'll be four o'clock in the morning. Change of plans, ladies. Kate, go back to your room and get some sleep. We'll do the same here. When we wake up, we'll try a few places and ask some questions. Shouldn't take long. How does that sound?"

"Okay, Sal. Then if all is fine, we can go get the trailer at the farmhouse with our belongings."

"Yes, and I feel better doing it this way, Kate. You had a great idea. One should always take safety precautions with strangers."

"Sal, we were almost strangers." Kate frowned.

"We were nearly strangers evacuating together, but we were also neighbors and went to the same church. It's not like we saw you and Ethan doing anything unusual where we'd put our family at risk by traveling with you two.

These are complete strangers, and in today's world, it's hard to trust strangers. What are they after? What's in it for them? What's their ulterior motive? You know what I'm trying to say?"

"I know, and you are right; there is a big difference between what our two families did together, and what these two men are supposedly offering. Let's pray about it, get some sleep, and check them out in the morning."

Sal yawned. "We'll see you much later today, Kate."

"Goodnight."

"Goodnight." They both said in unison as she made her way to the door and left.

Chapter Ten

Douglas entered the kitchen wearing Judy's royal blue satin robe. A twinkle of mischief shot from her narrowing eyes as she approached him.

"You look like a Hollywood movie star, shimmering around in satin…or should I say slinking around."

"A cigar would complete the image." He grinned. "But I never smoked cigars. Thankfully, I quit smoking cigarettes after my school years. I'd get bronchitis each time I'd sneak a smoke…be sick for weeks and go right back to it again."

"I remember." Judy nodded.

He rubbed his hand across his chin appearing deep in thought. Frowning, he continued.

"I finally cut back to one cigarette after each meal, then half a cigarette a day, and then I quit cold turkey. There, now you know my secret."

"Good for you, and good for me."

"Good for you?"

"Yes, you don't stink of stale cigarette smoke. The smell remains on you, your clothing, your house, your car..."

"Okay, I get it. Enough about cigarettes already."

"We do get carried away. Let's start over." She cleared her throat. "My, don't you look distinguished."

He sauntered closer to her.

"Is this a job interview? Do you need to review my work history?"

"Oh no, sir. This is simply an overdue haircut."

They laughed as she pulled a chair from the table and positioned it in the center of the room.

"Have a seat, please."

"Uh, yes, ma'am." He replied sharply; all signs of friendliness immediately left.

As she draped a towel over his shoulders, he glanced at the puzzled expression on her face. She sectioned off his hair with metal clips. Hair dropped to the floor as she cut with gusto. Douglas kicked his shoes into the pile of hair on the floor and frowned again. The moment did not pass unnoticed by Judy. She sucked her breath in and involuntarily shivered as tension grew between them.

The kitchen clock seemed to be ticking louder as they remained silent. Judy stopped occasionally to scoop hair off the floor and place it into a wastebasket.

"Douglas, are you okay?"

"Yeah. Why do you ask?"

"You don't seem like yourself. What made you so moody all of a sudden?"

"I have many sides you don't know about."

She leaned against his shoulder while tilting his head up.

He stiffened. She continued cutting. Clipping hair around his ears took longer as she compared each side to the other, then cutting and thinning the hair above his ears. Carefully running a comb through his hair, she nodded to herself and put the scissors on the table.

"All done."

"What about the beard?"

"I've never worked on a beard. No trimming, shaping; nothing. I haven't a clue on how to start removing your beard."

He stood and deliberately shook the loose hair from the towel, scattering clumps and wisps of hair over the entire kitchen.

"What did you do that for?" She shrieked. "I shake the towel outside, not in here."

"Calm down, woman. Let's start over again." He flung the towel back over his shoulders and returned to the chair sitting slumped with legs outstretched.

"Cut off the beard then I'll shave. You do have a razor, don't you?"

"Yes, but I don't share it."

"Well, there is a first time for…"

Judy interrupted him. "Douglas, I'll get you a throw-away razor I haven't used. It's a hygiene issue for me."

He shrugged. "Go get it then,

I'm not going anywhere."

Judy's face hardened. With her mouth drawn into a tight line, she went to the bathroom and gasped as she entered the room. Puddles of water were on the floor. Wet towels were discarded at random draping over the sink and toilet. Some lay wadded up on the floor.

She stepped over one and muttered to herself. "How much mess can one man make?"

Fuming, she retrieved the razor and marched back to the kitchen.

"Douglas, let's get one thing straight right now. I am not the maid. You make a mess; you clean it up."

"Now that's not much of a welcome, my dear." He grinned

again.

"Don't you 'my dear' me."

"You need something to ease your nerves. Here's the perfect pill for you." He reached into his pocket and opened a small prescription bottle of pills. He popped one in his mouth and handed her one.

"Come on, you're next."

"I don't take someone else's pills."

"Oh, that's right, you have your own." He laughed, and Judy stared at him wide-eyed.

"How do you know what I take?"

"Girl, it's common knowledge you are Bi-Polar. You are fine as long as you take your meds. What I have will relax you."

"Well, I'm not interested."

"I know something that is going to interest you."

"I don't know, Douglas. You have changed so much I hardly know why you're here. I thought you came to see me."

"Oh, I did, but I have a plan too. That's what I think you'll be interested in. My plan. And it's a sweet one too." He winked at her, and she caught herself backing away from him.

A loud buzzer suddenly went off in the distance and Judy bolted.

"The washer stopped. I'll put the clothes in the dryer."

Hurrying with her task, she returned and resumed cutting hair.

Her hands trembled as she snipped off the beard. Douglas grew unusually quiet again.

"Okay, the rest is up to you." She slid the razor towards him on the table. He strolled to the bathroom and still didn't speak.

Fidgeting with the scissors, she put them in a drawer and cleaned the kitchen.

After waiting in vain for his return, she stood still and listened. No sounds came from the bathroom. Throwing the dustpan and broom into the closet, she marched to the bathroom. The door suddenly opened, and he emerged. Clean-shaven? Yes. Clean appearance? No. He had the rough, blotchy face of someone she barely recognized. He even had a tattoo on his face, and another on his neck.

He passed her and silently returned to the kitchen. She followed.

Judy froze and studied him while he flopped into the chair sliding down on it, obviously trying to make himself comfortable.

"Douglas, you frighten me." She whispered.

"I was in prison. That's all it is. I think part of it goes everywhere I go."

"Do you want it to?"

He abruptly stood and leaned his face within inches of hers.

"What is this? A lecture on me?"

"No. I'm trying to be helpful, that's all."

"Well, if you want to be helpful, sit down and listen to my plan."

Chapter Eleven

Half-awake, Sal and his family climbed into the car. Carlos and Rosa stumbled over each other as both tried to enter at the same time.

"Hey, there is plenty of room, guys. Be careful."

"Sorry, Dad. Sorry, Rosa."

"Me too, Carlos."

Maria handed Rosa her stuffed teddy bear, and Rosa hugged it.

Kate waited as they fastened their seat belts. Yawning, she put the vehicle in reverse. Glancing at

Sal in the rear-view mirror, she paused before leaving the parking lot.

"What do you think about that family diner in town?"

"Good place to start asking questions."

"And we can eat while we're there." Maria gushed.

"Sounds good to me." Kate smiled to herself. "I prayed again this morning. Turned everything over to the Lord. I prayed for His will and His guidance in all we do. Prayed for healing for Ethan, and for our protection wherever we go." She flashed a genuine smile at the passengers in the back seat.

"We prayed too." Maria nodded.

"We are ready for today." Sal added as he petted the dog on his lap. Rufus rolled over on his back for a belly rub.

"This dog isn't a bit spoiled." Sal laughed.

"He is pure joy. Nothing can ruin your day when Rufus is around. He'll make you laugh at his antics." Kate replied.

"I feel like such a burden has been lifted off my shoulders. With God's guidance, we have a plan. Yes, Sal, we are ready for today."

"It frees you to receive His blessings. Our strong faith and His promises are soaring! Lead us on, Lord!" Maria sang out and lifted her hand in the air.

"Be careful, Mom. You almost

knocked me over." Rosa announced.

"Well, that's certainly not part of the plan."

Laughter erupted as the journey continued.

Chapter Twelve

Gina applied liquid soap on the wet paper towels and cleansed her body. She lathered the paper towels again for her daughter, Elsa. The two-year old held her tiny fingers under the running stream of water in the sink.

Gina had locked the door on the west wing public bathroom at Brooks Medical Center. Here, on the 7th floor, few employees, patients, or doctors were around to discover her. She let the toddler giggle and enjoy the cool water. Refreshed, Gina cleansed and dried off her daughter.

Brushing Elsa's hair first, she hurried to brush her own. It had been a blissful, safe night of undisturbed sleep. No looking over her shoulder, no crankiness from not enough sleep. Hospital bathrooms were a blessing in more ways than one.

She dug deep in the oversized shoulder purse and withdrew two cans of Vienna sausage, a small box of crackers, and a bottle of Pedialyte for Elsa. Gina filled her empty water bottle from the faucet and immediately drank most of it. She refilled it with the cool water.

Opening both cans of food, she placed one in front of Elsa and spread crackers out on a paper towel. The toddler clapped her hands in delight.

"Wieners..." She broke one in half trying to get it out of the can. Gina took some out and placed them next to the crackers. The little girl hummed while she ate. Gina sat the opened bottle of Pedialyte near the meal and Elsa gulped her favorite flavor, strawberry.

Taking a bite of cracker, Gina chewed it slowly and had another. Saving half of her can for Elsa, she also ate her Vienna sausage slowly.

The meal didn't last long, but it filled their hunger for a while. Gina reached back into her shoulder purse and retrieved spray body scent and deodorant. Using both sparingly on herself, she shoved all of their belongings back in the purse and threw their trash into the wastebasket. Gina grabbed her daughter and left the bathroom.

Walking down the long hallway, she encountered a nurse hurrying by. The tiled floor briefly echoed before the hallway emptied. Gina stopped at the elevator, and let Elsa punch the down button. Elsa clapped her hands again and giggled as the elevator whirled noisily to their floor.

"You are such a big girl." Gina hugged her.

"She sure is cute." An older woman's voice took Gina by surprise.

"Thank you, ma'am." Gina stammered and turned to face the older woman standing behind her.

"Are you from around here? I don't believe I've seen you before."

"Just passing through." Gina attempted a smile.

"Well, Crockett is a friendly small town. You'd feel welcome here. In fact, if you do decide to stay, I happen to know that Jarmann Market is hiring."

"Oh really? Where is it?"

"Leaving the hospital, it's three blocks to the right."

"My goodness, thanks for the tip. I might check it out."

"You're welcome. Have a good day." The woman waved at Elsa and with a slight limp continued on her way.

"You too." Gina watched the woman enter a patient's room two doors down. The elevator arrived unoccupied. Gina stepped inside and gazed at Elsa.

"Young lady, we are going to a market. This might be my answer to prayer. If not, we're getting closer to it. Either way, life is good."

Chapter Thirteen

Maria and the children continued eating the delicious meal. Kate asked the waitress for a refill on her coffee, and soon had a steaming hot cup of the fresh brew. Sipping it, she noticed several men at the counter conversing with each other. Sal raised an eyebrow at Kate and motioned toward the men. She nodded and continued sipping.

Sal eased out of his chair and approached them cautiously. "Morning, gentleman. Mind if I join you?"

"Always room for one more." A portly older man responded. "Haven't seen you around, you must be visiting someone."

Sal sprang onto the nearest bar stool.

"No sir. I'm not visiting. Looks like I got a great job offer yesterday. I'm Sal Hernandez, and I'll be working for Hubert and Monroe Chisum. Ever hear of them?"

"Hear of them? Why, they're from one of the oldest families to settle in this county. Good people, both of them. Hard-working. Honest. You couldn't find a more outstanding pair of brothers to work for."

"Well, thank you. I appreciate it. I didn't catch your name."

"Pardon my manners. I've got the cart before the horse." He laughed and extended his hand. "I'm Virgil Henry, and this is my fishing buddy, Ben Tyler."

Ben nodded as Sal shook hands with both men.

"Pleased to meet you." Sal seemed relieved and visibly relaxed.

"Likewise."

"So, you'll be working at the farm?" Virgil asked.

"Yes."

"You'll like working for them." Ben speculated.

"Any advice? Anyplace to recommend?" Sal edged off the barstool.

"Well...talk has it one of our old school chums is back from the big city. It's possible that he killed his wife. If you run into Ethan Meyers, I'd go in the opposite direction." Virgil replied solemnly. "We heard he is in the hospital, but don't know for how much longer."

"And stay away from the woman he's with now. She is a shady character if ever I heard of one." Ben spit tobacco juice in his paper cup. "She is feisty. Stirs up trouble."

"Well, thank you, I guess. I thought you'd recommend a church, or the best automotive repair shop or…"

"You've been warned. Believe me, your concern should be steering clear of both of them."

"Well, I guess you would know." Sal stepped forward to leave.

"I certainly do. My sister is Judy Harris. She knows all about them." Virgil grimaced.

"You gentlemen have a nice day. Thanks for the welcome."

Sal veered back to his table and discovered everyone had finished eating.

"Let's get out of here. Hurry, before they stop us and ask any more questions."

Kate gave Maria a quick glance and they left immediately. Sal paid the cashier and hurried them out the door.

"What happened?" Kate asked.

"Not now. Everyone in the car. Kate, you can drive us to the farmhouse to get the trailer. We'll talk on the way."

"So, the brothers turned out to be, okay?"

"Yes, Kate, the brothers did."

Chapter Fourteen

The tattoos on Douglas' face and neck seemed to grow uglier to Judy each time she saw them. She turned her head away from him as he spoke.

"The Meyers' homestead is vacant, and I intend to claim it's mine. I checked it out recently. It has great potential," Douglas announced.

Judy stared at the palms of her hands as the words fell from his mouth.

Another side of Douglas...this one is cold and arrogant...

"Are you listening to me?" He huffed and stood within inches of her face.

"I am thinking about the Meyers." She managed to say before biting down on her bottom lip.

"It can be done." Douglas snickered and crossed his arms. "I'll say I am related to the Meyers' family. Legally, as someone who murdered his wife, Ethan Meyers should be in prison for the rest of his life. With me having the right lawyer, he would no longer be entitled to the property. I can do it."

"I would love to see Ethan in prison for what he did to Becky." Judy stepped aside from Douglas making her way to a chair.

"Wouldn't you enjoy living out there?" He crooned and advanced closer glaring at her as she plopped into a chair.

"Yes, of course, Douglas. You know Ethan's in town, don't you?"

"In town?" Douglas blurted. "Where is he staying? He's definitely not at the family home."

"I talked to a policeman yesterday about Ethan," Judy cocked her eyebrow at him; "Douglas... Ethan's in the hospital here. Apparently unconscious. His supposedly new wife is not allowed to see him, as no one believes they are married. She may have tried to kill him." Judy added.

"She's after the property?" Douglas snarled as his face turned crimson red.

"I don't know," Judy whined with an emotion-choked voice. "And her name is Kate. All I know is she got kind of uppity with me when I talked to her the other day. They were trying to move in at his parents house. Kate wanted the electricity turned on, and I told her only Ethan could do that. Talk about huffy, and she doesn't know it's all over town she tried to do him in. Got what she deserved if you ask me."

"Who told you Kate couldn't see Ethan at the hospital?"

"Douglas, can we talk about something else?" Judy attempted to rise from her chair and almost lost her balance.

"No." He commanded in a loud voice, shoving her back onto the chair. Suddenly he leaned over her with his face next to hers. Baring his teeth, he breathed through his open mouth, and Judy cringed.

"Speak up, Judy. I want the rest of it."

She slumped in the chair and frowned. "The hospital security guard told me. He's a friend of my brothers."

Douglas cracked his knuckles and a vein twitched in his neck. "Okay, Judy." He spat. "I'll need to move in with you. No one will ever see me at your house, and no one can know about us yet. Later, yes, but not now. Understood? This is a pretty remote area. I won't be seen by anyone. I help you and you help me. What do you say?"

Judy tried to speak but choked on her words. Gasping, she tried to display calmness, yet her voice still quivered with fear. "Douglas, what if you can't...can't get your lawyer to believe you?"

"Oh, he will. He owes me a favor." He flashed Judy a fake smile. "Can you imagine living there? And not paying rent anymore? Leasing out the pastures will bring in more than enough income to support us and pay both insurance and taxes."

"You've thought this out for a long time, haven't you, Douglas?"

"Years in prison can be productive. I have the plan of a lifetime, Judy. Let's do this."

She nodded.

"And I can move in with you?"

Judy nodded again.

His attitude instantly changed. Dreamy-eyed, he kissed her slowly on her lips.

"There." He said in a gravelly voice. "Sealed with a kiss."

No…sealed with the effects of your pill…

She rose from her chair and broke out in a cold sweat.

His plan truly is evil…

Chapter Fifteen

Gina held Elsa on the side of her hip as she entered the market. A few customers were standing in line waiting to be checked out. Others were ambling up and down the aisles carrying items in a plastic basket. Many talked to each other as they shopped. Elsa eagerly reached for everything they walked past. Leaning over, she almost tumbled out of Gina's arms and giggled.

"That's not funny, Elsa."

"She is determined to get down."

Gina whirled, nearly falling into a tall man about her own age.

"Oh, I'm sorry. I didn't see you. Yes, she is determined." Gina laughed.

"Are you finding everything alright? Can I help with something?"

"Do you work here?"

"Uh, yes. Yes, I do."

"I'm looking for the manager's office. I heard they were hiring here."

"They are hiring. Let me show you to the office...right this way."

Gina followed him around the corner and down another aisle before reaching their destination. The office had large plate glass windows across the front. She observed another man working behind a desk. The employee opened the door for her and escorted her inside.

"Kurt, this lady is looking for a job."

He stood immediately. "Kurt Schuhmacher, and we are needing a bookkeeper. Have you any experience?"

"...Yes." She instantly did a double-take at the other man as both men burst out laughing.

"Happens all the time. We are identical twins. I'm Kurt, and this is my brother Karl."

"I've never met identical twins before. It would be difficult to tell you apart. I'm Gina."

"Please, sit down. And who is this little girl wiggling in your arms?" Kurt pulled a chair to the front of the desk. Gina took it and gingerly sat with the child.

"This is my daughter, Elsa."

Karl sucked in his breath and glanced at his brother.

"We don't hear that name often." Kurt smiled.

"And it's special to us, you see, it's our mother's name. German names aren't that common here." Karl added.

"Well, meet Elsa Sehlke. We Sehlke's are definitely German." Gina grinned.

"And she's definitely adorable. Mother will have to meet her." Karl reached for his cell phone and texted someone. "Please, excuse my manners. May I get you something to drink? Coffee? Water?"

"Oh no, thank you. I'm fine."

"Mother is coming. She is the boss." Kurt spoke in a caring tone. "She will interview you and explain the details."

Elsa managed to free herself from her mother's grasp, and Gina grabbed her as the office door opened.

Mrs. Schuhmacher entered the room and stared straight at Elsa. "Look at those long curls. My goodness, what a pretty little girl."

"Mother, this is Gina Sehlke and her daughter, Elsa. Gina is looking for a job."

"Nice to meet you, Mrs. Sehlke, or is it Ms.?"

"Either will work with me, I'm widowed."

"Oh, my. You are so young to be widowed. My condolences." She pulled a chair closer to Gina. "Are you familiar with bookkeeping? Any experience?"

"I worked for the Ammerman & Moseley CPA firm for four years in Ft. Leavenworth, Kansas. That's where my husband died. I've been traveling since. I guess you could say I'm looking for a place to settle."

"Do you have relatives here?"

"No ma'am, I don't."

"It must be hard on you raising your daughter alone."

"Oh no, ma'am. She's a lot of company to me."

"I'm sure she is. I tell you what, young lady. I like you, and I like your determination."

Karl interrupted. "Gina's daughter gets that from her." He grinned.

Gina gave him a slight smile.

"I'll contact the CPA firm for your work record and get back to you this afternoon. If all looks promising, you can start tomorrow morning at nine o'clock. I pay $14.00 an hour, 40-hour weeks, off Sunday and Monday. One week vacation a year, and some insurance benefits. After your first two weeks, I'll cover what insurance you'll qualify for. Fair enough?"

"Yes, and I'll take it. I do need a babysitter though. Is there anyone you could recommend?"

"I'm not aware of anyone, but I think between myself, Kurt, and

Karl we could take turns until someone is found."

"You'd do that for me? Oh, thank you, Mrs. Schuhmacher." Gina's eyes watered, and she quickly glanced down at Elsa.

Stop it…don't cry…that's not professional…

Taking a deep breath, Gina regained her composure and stood to leave. Elsa ran to Mrs. Schuhmacher and hugged her legs.

"Tell her bye."

"Bye." Elsa squealed and happily ran back to Gina.

"Thanks again… to all of you." Gina reached the door and Mrs. Schuhmacher called out anxiously. "Wait. I didn't get your phone number."

"I don't have one. I'll come back at about four o'clock. Hopefully, you'll know something by then." Gina didn't give the woman a chance to reply. She sailed out the door and left the market. Once outside, she grabbed little Elsa's hands.

"Happy dance, let's do a happy dance."

The child's laughter filled the air as they spun around holding hands enjoying their happy dance. Gina's face glowed with pure joy.

Karl happened to look out the window and spotted them. His eyes crinkled with merriment, and he knew he'd never be able to think or talk about anything else.

Chapter Sixteen

"I don't know if I can take being at the farmhouse without Ethan." Kate said half-aloud as she drove.

"Ethan would want you to, and we have to get that trailer with our belongings in it. I don't know about you, but these clothes we're wearing need to be changed...and pretty soon." Maria chuckled.

"You are right. Besides, I can't wait to see the new place."

"Me too." Sal cleared his throat. "I think we'll all be busy getting situated and into a routine."

"As soon as we get the trailer, I'm making calls for help with my marriage license. Keep praying. It's

163

still early in the morning. Progress could be right around the corner."

Sal seemed to perk up after hearing Kates's positive viewpoint.

"What did the men at the diner say?" Maria glanced at her husband.

"Oh, they thought highly of the Chisum brothers, but…" He coughed and frowned at Maria.

"But what?" Kate asked from the front seat.

Sal hung his head. "You know I can't stand gossip. They were like parrots repeating stuff Judy Harris said."

"Judy Harris? What's she got to do with this?"

"Kate, she is the sister of one of those men."

"She's not a sister to the Chisum brothers, is she?"

"No, Kate, she's a sister to one of the men I talked to at the diner."

"Oh, well, I won't put up with her or let her ruin my day. 'I can do all things through Christ who strengthens me.' That's Philippians 4:13, one of my favorite scriptures."

"Mine too. I just don't want her causing us any trouble. We've had enough." Sal peered at Maria and frowned again. She immediately gave him a puzzling stare and raised her eyebrows in a questioning expression. Sal looked her in the eye and grimaced.

"There's more going on, isn't it?" Maria whispered to Sal.

He merely nodded and quickly turned his head to gaze out the window.

Barely audible even to Sal, Maria prayed in earnest. He patted her shoulder and also prayed quietly while he viewed the countryside passing by.

"I'm driving right toward the sun; I need my sunglasses. I left them at the farmhouse though." Kate blinked and rubbed her eyes. "Maybe it won't be long, and we can watch the sunrise from there." She laughed. "At this point, I don't care which farmhouse it is, Ethans, or the Chisum's."

"Kate, you know you do care, and stop calling it Ethans. It's yours too."

"I know, Maria. I guess it's a habit of calling the farmhouse Ethans. He grew up there, and I have special feelings for it too. Listening to his stories helps me picture him as a young boy and visualize how he enjoyed living there. It's like going back in time and feeling what he did with each new experience."

"I've even heard some of his stories. He told me how he and his dog ran all over the pastures playing ball." Sal said.

"So many memories. I remember the story he told about the first time he cleaned fish, and how his dog ran off with the biggest one." Kate added.

"He can surely tell a story." Sal laughed.

Kate turned off the main road, continued driving, and lowered the windows. She glanced at the Hernandez family in the back seat.

"Am I the only one that enjoys hearing the crunch of the gravel on this road?" She smiled.

"We love it." Maria answered.

"I call it an overwhelming dose of country living." Kate kept her smile as she drove.

The farmhouse came into view minus all the loose cattle they'd seen on their first trip. It seemed quiet and peaceful. As Kate pulled into the front of the house, Sal leaned forward.

"I'll back the car up to the trailer if you'll guide me to the trailer hitch."

"That's a deal."

She jumped out and walked to the front of the trailer.

Sal got behind the steering wheel and slowly backed the car toward her. Kate motioned for him to ease toward the right. He did and carefully continued. She raised her arm straight into the air as he got close enough to the hitch.

"Stop."

Sal left the car and examined how the car lined up with the trailer hitch.

"Good job, Kate."

He lowered the jack on the trailer, and the metal ball protruding behind the car slid directly into the hitch of the trailer. He secured it and nodded.

"We're good to go."

Kate scowled. "Do you think we should inspect the place before we leave?"

"No. We need to get out of here now. We could have interrupted anything when we arrived. Someone or some people could be hiding."

"Well, the police have it under surveillance. We got what we came for." Kate took a deep breath.

Sal edged toward the car. "I'll drive in case we get followed. Just a safety precaution. Come on."

Kate squinted as she climbed in the passenger's side of the front seat. She gave one lingering look at the house and pasture and involuntarily shivered.

Sal turned the car and trailer around and headed out. As he drove under the massive archway with MEYERS spaced evenly across it, he stopped and got out.

"What is it?" Kate and Maria yelled.

"A mangled drone. I didn't see it when we came through the entrance a while ago." He shoved windblown hair from his forehead and got back in the car.

"Did any of you see it?" He asked.

"No."

"I didn't."

"We didn't either, Daddy."

Sal laughed. "Oh well. It could have run into a tree. Don't worry about it."

"No worries here." Kate glanced at Maria and offered a thumbs up. Maria smiled warmly returning the gesture.

Sal drove off and the silence seemed soothing.

Before leaving the gravel road he pulled over and set the GPS to the Chisum's farmhouse. Carlos and Rosa played with Rufus and in all appearances, everyone enjoyed a pleasant trip.

Sal observed his surroundings and periodically glanced at the road behind him. No traffic, and no, they weren't being followed. His passengers catnapped while he drove the hour and a half to their destination. When the GPS announced they had arrived, Sal could only see farmland. No houses, and no buildings. He finally noticed a sign near the exit of the main road, simply stating, "Chisum & Company, *Established 1897*"

Pressing harder on the gas pedal, he entered the Chisum property. "Wake up. We're here." His voice rang out as he lowered the windows to once again enjoy the full effect of the country.

Startled, everyone stirred from leaning on each other in the backseat and stared out the windows. A wooded area obviously decades-old grew on both sides of the road. Trees and overgrown brush were so thick you couldn't see through them.

Kate's mouth dropped open as they rounded a corner. "Wow. Look at that…"

A sprawling compound, the Chisum's farmhouse sat in the middle of acres of pasture. Not a barn a typical city dweller would imagine. No quaint red barn with chickens pecking at the surrounding dirt.

A two-story, industrial building housing enormous farm equipment. Modern? Indeed.

"Where is everybody?" Carlos asked as he scanned the area.

"Probably working in some field, son." Sal continued driving and spotted another sign. This one stated 'OFFICE' with a red arrow pointing behind the building.

Driving behind the massive building, they discovered an

awesome panoramic sight. A beautiful wide, blue and white sky accented the Chisum settlement set in a valley basking in sunshine and gentle breezes.

Kate and the Hernandez family gasped and seemed awestruck.

A tall, metal horse barn and an equally tall, open-air hay barn were about fifty feet from each other. The office building, also a tall metal building, sat apart from the others.

Another building, not as tall, had large glass windows and had adjoining sidewalks to the office building. Unusually narrow, its dimensions ranged approximately forty feet wide and about eighty feet long. The last building set further away from the others displayed a healthy small garden on the right side.

The roads connecting these buildings had rutted tracks from farm tractors and vehicles that cut through to the pastures.

Sal maneuvered the car to the office building and parked.

"Stay here. I'll check this out."

He noticed a huge, modern home even farther back from the buildings as he walked to the office. Still staring at the house, Sal didn't notice the office door open. He turned, and nearly bumped into Monroe Chisum.

Monroe, with a wide grin, offered Sal his hand and Sal promptly shook it.

"Welcome. I watched you drive-in. Have any trouble finding the place?"

"No, none at all."

"Well, that's where you'll be staying." He pointed to the building with a garden. He handed Sal a key. "And that's where you'll be working." Monroe motioned to the narrow building next door.

"I'll be glad to unload and get settled..." Sal began.

Monroe stopped him. "How are you doing? I mean, do you need an advance to buy groceries or anything?"

"Oh, no. We're fine. I do appreciate it, though. Exceedingly kind of you." Sal's voice filled with emotion.

"No problem. Go ahead and unpack. I won't keep you. Come see me here at eight in the morning, and I'll show you your job duties. You'll get paid at the end of each week."

"Fair enough." Sal nodded and walked back to the car.

Monroe remained standing in front of the office door. "Oh, by the way. About your job…you'll be removing the faces off of cheap, oversized clocks and…"

Startled, Sal turned and interrupted Monroe. "Clocks?"

"Yes." Monroe shifted his weight to his left hip and leaned against the doorframe. "You'll reassemble a new face with glow-in-the-dark numbers that you'll paint on with stencils."

"And paint with stencils, oh boy." Sal grinned and shook his head in disbelief. "Don't think I'm not happy to get the job, I am. I can do it with practice."

Monroes face lit up with a wide smile. "You can learn, and stencil painting can be a surprising new skill."

Sal laughed wholeheartedly and opened the driver's door.

"Yes sir, Mr. Chisum. It might even surprise me, but I'll give it my best effort."

Monroe nodded and returned to the office.

Sal eased behind the steering wheel and drove off to the building with the garden, still grinning.

Chapter Seventeen

Judy stared in defiance at Douglas and wrinkled her brow.

"I understand why you want the Meyers property, but why do you need my help?"

"Why? You ask me why? Judy, you have contacts in this town. Everyone in Crockett listens to every word you speak. And you are so believable. No matter what you say, it is considered the truth."

Judy tilted her head and fluttered her long, fake eyelashes. "Are you saying I have a way with words?" She pouted her lips.

"Yes, and you know it. Now, stop flirting. Listen to me. This is serious."

He grabbed her by her shoulders and physically sat her in a chair.

"Stop it." She snarled.

"Then you stop it."

"Alright already."

"That's better. Now I want you to go shopping and buy me some decent clothes. I'll give you a list of what I want and the sizes."

"And how am I supposed to pay for all of this?"

"I can pay for it. I've been saving for a long time. They don't pay much for work in prison, but I sold my art and craft projects. Turns out I'm extremely talented in woodwork and a perfectionist at details."

"What a shame it took being in prison for you to discover your talent. You could be self-employed by now with your own shop…not to mention mail order."

"I have a talent. It supported me well. I happened to have broken into the wrong establishment that had hidden cameras."

"I don't agree with that. You got what you deserved. If I had worked hard to build a business, get credit, and pay off loans; I would hide cameras to protect my business like that guy did. You can't expect to live off of others all your life, Douglas."

"Whose side are you on?" He demanded. "You have gone too far this time."

Judy raised mid-way from her chair, and he clenched his teeth while shoving her down.

Her face flushed and she jabbered non-stop. "I referred to what I'd do if I had a business and got robbed. I can't help it if you chose to do that to someone. Your decision and your actions cost you time in prison. No one forced you. No one else is to blame. Now, stop it." She attempted to stand, and he stepped to the side.

"Get me a pen and paper." He snarled.

Judy walked to a drawer and retrieved both. Handing the items to him, she gasped at the loud sound of each inhale and exhale he took. He obviously could not hide his rage.

Douglas scribbled the clothing, shoe items, and the sizes with colors and styles he preferred. He laid the paper on the table and patted it with his hand.

"Do not mess this up. At all. Do you understand?"

"Of course." She breathed.

He pulled several hundred-dollar bills from a dirty sock he hid in the pocket of the robe he wore.

"Here. This should be enough."

"You want me to go now?" Judy asked incredibly.

"Yes, Judy, now. And wherever you go, I want you to spread gossip…"

"Spread gossip? What gossip?" Judy blurted.

"Make up lies, discredit, put them down, talk trashy; whatever term you wish to call it; but you are to talk against Ethan, and what's her name?"

"Kate. Her name is Kate."

"You talk against Ethan and Kate. I don't want anyone to trust either of them. They will be the bad guys in this town. You got it?"

"I got it. But what will I say?"

"Whatever it takes."

Chapter Eighteen

Gina returned to the Jarmann Market a few minutes before four o'clock that evening. Elsa clapped her hands as they entered, obviously remembering her earlier visit. Gina veered around several people and with an alert gaze searched for either Karl or Kurt. She saw only one employee, a middle-aged woman who worked the checkout counter and had a long line of customers patiently waiting for their turn.

Not wanting to interrupt her, Gina strolled down the aisles, but all in vain. Finding neither twin, she sighed and went to the office.

She didn't see anyone there

and walked closer to the glass windows. She noticed ledger books and papers scattered over the floor in front of a desk.

Strange...maybe Mrs. Schuhmacher had a heart attack, or someone had to be rushed to the hospital or...

Gina darted back to the checkout counter. A customer chatted on a personal level with the cashier. Another customer in line chimed in.

The cashier tried to keep the line flowing as they discussed the new positions taken by the school board on discipline. Pros and cons grew louder as the customers voiced their opinions. Opinions soon grew into heated arguments and politeness turned into ranted rude remarks.

One woman yelled, "If you'd raise your children to be accountable for their actions…"

Another shouted, "I don't enable my teens…"

Visibly upset, the cashier stopped working. "Ladies, please, this isn't the place for this type of encounter."

"Well, why not? I have a right to voice my opinion."

The cashier nodded. "Yes, and I'm working here until nine o'clock. You are interfering with my pleasant work environment. You are making me nervous."

"Pleasant work environment? What happened to the customer is always right? You obviously don't want repeat customers. Well, I won't be back." The angry woman threw her loaf of bread and other items on top of the candy rack and walked out.

The remaining customers looked wide-eyed at each other, and the cashier hurried to check them out. She sighed when the last one left.

Gina gave a timid smile.

"That almost got out of hand."

The cashier laughed. "I've never checked out so many people that fast in my life. I'm Sheila, can I help you find something?"

"Yes, and I'm Gina. I had an appointment to meet the Schuhmachers today at four o'clock. I'm worried. It's four o'clock, and they aren't here." Gina's voice rose to a high pitch.

Elsa, feeling her mother's anxiety immediately started squirming in her arms and whimpering.

"I don't know where they are, but I'm sure they'll return soon. I was busy with customers when they rushed out of the store. They assured me they'd be right back. Sorry, I can't be of any more help. Now, if there's nothing else…"

"Oh, no, thank you."

Gina watched her greet other customers.

Leaving the store, she tried to hush her fussy daughter.

I hate to walk back to the hospital and sit in the waiting room, but I guess I have no choice…

People were scattered along the sidewalk. She dodged those who wouldn't move over. Increasing her pace, Gina sang a lullaby to her daughter and Elsa's whining slowed. One couple walking toward her smiled at Elsa as they ambled by. Further away, a police officer approached, and Gina stepped to one side letting him pass. He raised his head at them making quick eye contact and rushed off down the sidewalk.

What is that all about? I don't even see his patrol car anywhere...

Elsa whimpered and yawned, clutching a handful of Gina's hair as they bobbed along to the hospital. Gina's shoes were worn, and their arch support had caved in weeks ago. Her feet ached. She shifted the weight of her daughter to her other side and stepped lightly. Elsa fussed louder.

And you, little one, need a nap…and so do I.

Chapter Nineteen

Sal and Maria appeared overwhelmed at the boxes and suitcases that lay fallen on the floor of the U-Haul trailer. Kate located her overnight bags and set them out on the ground.

"Let's leave the large boxes for later." Kate glanced at the couple. "I already owe a late charge for returning the trailer. One more day can't be much worse."

"Okay with me." Sal jumped into the trailer and glanced at the mess.

"You two ladies stay where you are, and I'll hand you what I recognize."

An hour later, with the trailer half emptied, they locked it and parked it near the front door. Placing baggage and small boxes in the correct bedrooms took time. Sal rubbed his back while Maria corralled the children.

"No running in this house. I'll take you for a walk after we rest."

Sal nodded at her as he walked to the kitchen. Opening the refrigerator, his voice rose with excitement. "Hey, we have sliced fruit and vegetable trays to snack on, and cheese and lunch meat." He poked at the deli selections. Bottled water and cans of soda were on another shelf. He closed the fridge. "Probably some crackers and bread around here somewhere. Mr. Chisum didn't have to do this, but I'm glad he did.

I don't feel like driving back to town for a fast-food meal or buying groceries."

"Mr. Monroe is kind, indeed."

Kate heard the chatter and plopped on a couch.

"I'll join you in a minute. Got to make some calls."

She grabbed her smartphone and held it in mid-air.

Now, where do I have my marriage license faxed to once it is copied and paid for? Do I trust the hospital? What about the police station? Or maybe both? Yes, that's it. Send it to both places…

Kate jotted down both fax numbers after a quick search using her phone. Taking a deep breath, she punched in the number for the Harris County Courthouse in Houston, Texas. Making her selection through an automated menu; she gave her information, request, and paid for the transaction by credit card. The monotone voice gave a confirmation number and stated the copies would be faxed within twenty-four hours.

She lazily stretched out on the couch, rolled over, and yawned. Lingering as long as possible, she finally got up and entered the kitchen. Unruly hair spiked at odd intervals across her forehead with some hanging over her eyes.

"What got a hold of you?" Maria chuckled as she bounced from her chair and hugged Kate warmly.

Kate shoved her hair back from her face and yawned again. Noticing her friend's bloodshot eyes, she shook her head.

"I think we all need a nap. No razzle-dazzle energy for me today. I'm frazzled and fried, but good news...the copies of my marriage license will be faxed in a matter of hours, not days. Hours, who would have guessed?"

"Thank You Lord Jesus." Maria beamed.

"Amen to that." Sal replied.

"Yes, it is a blessing. Thank You Heavenly Father for taking care of that burden. I can't wait to see Ethan." She sighed and looked at the snacks Sal had placed on the table. "And thank You Heavenly

Father for this food." She added.

Each opened their drink and dove into the food trays.

"I don't think any of us slept much last night. I know I didn't." Kate munched on a turkey breast and cheddar cheese sandwich.

"Umm. You can tell this is Sargento's cheese. It's real cheese…delicious." Kate savored the bite, then took a drink of ice-cold water from the bottle.

"It's the only cheese I buy." Maria nodded.

"Can we go for a walk now?" Carlos asked.

"Can we please, Momma?" Rosa, wide-eyed, stopped eating and gazed at her mother.

"After we eat and get unpacked."

Both of the children took huge bites and swung their legs in anticipation.

"Can we walk to the barn? I want to see horses." Rosa wiggled in her chair.

"I don't think all barns have horses, Rosa." Maria chuckled.

"Ms. Kate, will you go too?"

Sal tossed his empty soda can into the trash container. "Carlos, Ms. Kate is tired. We'll go soon."

Kate regarded his invitation. "No, Carlos, but Rufus would love to go. You have to keep him on his leash, though."

"Okay. I will do it." He solemnly replied.

"Knock on my door when you're ready for Rufus. Now, if you will excuse me, I'm going to unpack and try out the queen-size bed in my room. It's certainly a huge bonus to have this place furnished." She sighed and eased out of her chair. Kates's face flushed as she turned and left.

"We won't be that long in getting Rufus," Maria called out as she returned the food trays to the refrigerator and cleaned off the table. Placing the bread and crackers in the cabinet, she sensed Kates's weariness, both physical and emotional.

"I'll unpack our clothes and put them where they belong, and hey, I'll even get the dog. Sal, could you put what we need in the bathroom? And get the coffee pot?"

"Sure, but only for you." His eyes sparkled as he fled whistling.

"You are crazy, Sal." She stifled a laugh and hurried on her way.

Maria completed her tasks first and returned to the kitchen with Rufus straining on the leash to go.

"Yea!" Carlos and Rosa ran to the feisty dog and patted him while he pranced.

"Sal? We're ready. Come on."

"I'm coming. I found all of the stuff."

He arrived out of breath, holding the electric coffee pot against his chest with his hand over it, and the coffee, dry coffee creamer, and sugar secured by his arm to his left side. Maria unloaded the supplies and set them on the counter. Opening a cabinet door, she withdrew three cups and placed them by the coffee pot.

"Let's go. I'll prepare the morning coffee when we get back."

Carlos and Rufus led the way, and as everyone darted out, Sal hurried to lock the door behind him. Once outside, each person paused to scan a different direction. Greeted by a blast of fresh air, the smell of sun-warmed earth mixed with the faint aroma of blooming wildflowers.

"I can't get enough of this." Sal took a deep breath.

"Me too." Maria stated.

A moment to savor; no one

moved except Rufus. His prancing increased.

"My goodness, you'd think none of us had been outside before." Maria teased.

The children giggled and raced off with the dog leading the way.

Carlos tugged at Rufus to slow him. "I'm walking you, Rufus. You aren't walking me." Carlos reached down and patted him. Rufus responded by sitting and panting. "Where to?" Carlos looked at his dad.

"Your sister wants to check out the barn."

"Yes, they might have horses." She squealed.

"Okay. I think Rufus has rested enough. Come on, boy."

Carlos, Rufus, and Rosa bounced along in front of Sal and Maria. Sal slipped his hand into Maria's.

"This walk is a great idea." He shaded his eyes from the sun's glare and spotted tractors with various farm equipment working distant fields. Dust plumes rose behind the machinery against a blue sky scattered with wisps of white clouds.

"So peaceful." She muttered.

Set to a leisure pace, they ambled toward the barn. Rosa stopped at the first sound of animals neighing.

"Horses." She whispered, her face beaming.

As they approached the barn

entrance, they listened to hooves pawing at the dirt and grass being ripped up and chewed. Rosa waited for her parents, and they entered as a group.

"We can watch, but don't disturb them." Maria warned.

The barn had twelve horses, each inside their own stall. All of the horses noticed the family entering the barn, but one in particular stood out from the rest. It physically turned and watched them enter and lifted its head as it whinnied. They went straight to the horse.

A mare. She whinnied and swished her tail as they edged toward her stall.

Sal flinched as they heard a

sharp crackle sound. An older man stood from his former bent position of spreading dry straw in a stall. "You must be the Hernandez family. Mr. Chisum said you'd be arriving today. I'm Clayton Fugler."

"Yes, we are. I'm Sal." He gulped and motioned with his hand, "my wife Maria, and these are our children, Carlos and Rosa. Nice to meet you."

"My pleasure."

"Mama, can I touch her? Please? I'll be quiet, and I won't scare her."

"I know you won't, sweetheart, but I don't know if the horse will be nice to you." Maria frowned.

"The mare's name is Precious.

She's gentle. The child won't be harmed. Go on and pet her."

Sal scooped up his daughter and carried her to the mare. Rosa trembled as she placed her tiny hand on the horse's neck. Precious rubbed her neck against Rosa's arm and whinnied again.

"She likes me, Daddy. She does." Rosa slowly caressed the horse with longer strokes until she no longer trembled.

"I think you have a new friend, Rosa."

"I do." She twisted to one side and pointed at Carlos. "Your turn."

He handed Rufus's leash over to his mother and made rapid strides to the horse stall.

Taking a deep breath, he softly talked to the mare. "Hello, Precious. You are beautiful, did you know that? Well, I think you are, and you know what? My sister will talk to you all day long if we let her." He carefully stroked her neck as he talked and Precious leaned toward him whinnying again.

"Tell Precious bye, we have to finish our walk." Sal interrupted.

Carlos continued his soft conversation with Precious. "And you know what? After our walk, someone is going to fall asleep in his recliner today."

Sal gave his son a half-smile and pointed to the open barn door.

"Thanks for the tip about the mare, Mr. Fugler."

"You're welcome, and come back, anytime."

They wandered out of the barn and strolled by the nearest building. An open-air hay barn stacked with square bales the length of the building had a scent all of its own. Workers were busy unloading a long trailer of freshly baled hay to another area.

"Can you smell that?" Sal stopped and took another deep breath.

Several men turned upon hearing Sal. Most continued working, but one nodded at Sal.

"That's sweet-smelling timothy hay. Nothing like it." He wiped the sweat off his brow and pitched another square bale off the trailer.

Sal gave him a thumbs-up hand sign and left with his family. Veering towards another building, the only occupants to be seen were definitely not working.

"Look at that." Maria laughed.

Cats were lying stretched out in the sun. Some slept near the side of the road, and some on the shady concrete sidewalk. Those who were wide awake appeared simply lazy.

Rufus charged with full force rearing his front legs up in the air.

A tabby, a calico, a solid black cat, and a grey striped cat with a bobbed tail took off in a flash escaping under the front porch.

"Keep Rufus away, Carlos. I don't want any pet hurt by

someone else's pet. Take Rufus back to Kate and tell her what happened. We're coming right behind you."

"Why do they have so many cats, Daddy? Do cats have cat friends?"

"Rosa, farmers keep cats to eat mice and scare snakes away. This must be siesta time. Come on, let's leave them alone. They are too scared to be petted anyway."

Maria latched onto Sal's hand again as they strolled to the new home. "Certainly, frightening for the cats, but …here we are relaxing, and…"

"And what Maria?"

"Still no word on Ethan's

condition. Kate can't keep struggling like this. Things are getting beyond scary for Kate and Ethan..."

"We'll keep praying."

Chapter Twenty

Kate opened her eyes and saw daylight. She lay in bed for a moment. Groggy, she remained still. Tossing and turning robbed her of too much sleep. With a slight moan, she stretched.

I have to check on Ethan…somehow…and check if the hospital or police station received copies of my marriage license…check to see if I have enough gas in the car…check to see if Rufus had a bathroom accident being in a new place and all…and take him outside…ask the police for an update of the surveillance on Ethan's farmhouse…

Thoughts continued to flood her mind as she remained sprawled in the bed.

But first, I'm praying again; Dear God, I pray for healing for Ethan, for Your Guidance and Your will in my life, for daily safe travel and protection for the Hernandez family and myself. I turn my burdens over to You and do not take them back. With my faith and trust in You, I am thankful You fight my battles. I stand on Your Word that no weapon formed against me shall prosper in Isaiah 54:17. Help me be a light for You in the midst of all this turmoil and darkness. I pray Your love and kindness will shine through me to others. Thank you for supplying all my needs. Please forgive me of my sins, and I forgive all others for anything they may have said or done against me. I pray that my enemies will come to know Jesus as their Savior. In Jesus' name, I pray, Amen.

Kate's feet hit the floor and she immediately went to the window. Opening the blinds, she smiled as the morning sunshine spread across the valley.

Now, I'm ready for the day…

A quick change of clothes, and she charged outside with Rufus. He had behaved himself in the new home last night, but she had to be on the lookout for cats.

I don't think he'd ever seen one before yesterday's encounter. Being afraid and trying to be dominant at the same time didn't work well for Rufus. Carlos said Rufus went from being sweet and happy to a furious angry animal. Hmm, it's the animal instinct to fear and the human instinct to defend…similar characteristics…anger management is available for humans, behavior school for dogs…but we were made in God's image with a soul…

Kate dismissed her thoughts as Rufus returned to her from doing his business. He snuggled against her legs, and she bent down, giving him a hug.

"Good boy, Rufus." Hurrying back to her room, she refilled his two metal bowls with fresh water and food. Patting him lovingly, she locked the door and left.

In the kitchen, she found Maria quietly enjoying her morning coffee.

"Mind if I join you?" Kate smiled again.

"Please do. Sal has left for work, and the children are sleeping late." She paused. "You certainly look refreshed. I worried about you, but a good night's sleep seems to have helped."

"I got some sleep, and I prayed sincerely earlier. Such a relief to turn everything over to God."

"A good way to start and end the day. We also have daily prayers."

Kate nodded and poured herself a steaming cup of coffee. "I'm leaving in a few minutes to try and see Ethan. Need anything while I'm in town?"

"No, but thanks."

Taking a chair at the table, she hesitated and bit on her bottom lip. "Maria, can I ask you a strange question?"

"Yes, and there is no such thing as a strange question...it's an intelligent search for finding out the truth of something."

Kate blew on the hot liquid and made eye contact with her friend while glancing over the rim of the cup. "Do you think animals go to heaven?"

Maria leaned forward in her chair and shrugged her shoulders. "Whatever made you think about that?"

"Rufus and the cats, and what almost happened. Thankfully, he didn't break loose from his leash, and the cats weren't injured or killed. I know some people like to picture the pets they had in the past waiting in Heaven for them when they arrive. I wondered if they do."

"That's a pretty deep subject. If God wants animals in heaven, I'm sure they will be there. But they were not made as we are. They can be taught a lot of things, but they cannot choose a life where the results of their actions will be heaven and hell. They are animals. There are work animals and pet animals. We were made in the image of God. They were not. Does this help?" She sighed.

"I guess. So, unless God wants them there, they won't be there. They were not made with a soul.

Only God's creations with a soul can go to heaven."

"That's what my teacher taught us in Sunday School, but Kate, look it up in the Bible. I use the King James Version. That'll be a great topic to research."

"Thanks for the suggestion. I will. I am curious." She smiled again. "By the way, Rufus will stay in my room. He has food and water and has already been out this morning. I'll be back by lunch to take him out. I can't wait to get to the hospital."

"I understand. Call me when you can."

"Of course." Kate stood from the table and winked at her friend. "This may be the day I get to see

Ethan." She sailed out the door obviously in a better mood.

Walking to the car, she recognized Mr. Monroe Chisum poking his head out the door of the nearby building.

"Good morning, ma'am." He remarked and waved at her.

"Good morning." She flashed him a smile and escaped into her car.

He must see everything that goes on by the window…stop it, now, be nice…he's probably bored…

Kate sighed and glanced at the gas gauge.

Hmm, full tank of gas…thank you, Sal!

She drove to the hospital and found a parking space. Bolting from the vehicle, she went inside, going straight to the crowded information desk. Waiting for her turn, she spoke in a friendly tone.

"Hi, I'm Kate Meyers. I'm hoping to see my husband today."

"I'm aware of who you are, and you are not allowed to see your husband until my supervisor approves it." The woman huffed and displayed an ugly frown.

Kate watched as the woman's frown deepened as she turned to answer the phone. Still agitated, she spoke sharply to whoever happened to be on the line and ended the call.

"Ma'am, you should have received the fax from the Harris County Courthouse by now. It's being sent to the Administration's Office."

The employee ignored Kate and typed something on her desk computer.

Kate stood at the counter as all eyes in the waiting room remained on her. Conversation ceased except for Kate's one-sided discussion.

"Would you please contact the Administrator and see if the fax came in?"

"She won't be in for thirty more minutes."

"Thank you, I'll wait."

Kate pivoted and noticed the waiting room had several people. A few of them smiled at her, which she likewise did in return; others stared ahead with a blank look on their face. Finding an empty group of chairs near a wall, Kate sat facing the entrance. Occasionally, she'd glance at her wristwatch. Five minutes, ten, then twenty went by. Another ten minutes. Another five minutes, still no one entered the hospital.

Kate slowly rose and approached the information desk again.

"Ma'am?"

"She must have some errands; she will be here though."

Returning to her chair, she watched a young woman leave the waiting room and walk down the adjoining hallway. A little girl bounced along beside her humming a song.

Later, a doctor in scrubs arrived calling out a family's last name. A couple jumped and ran towards him as he assured them their relative's surgery went well and explained that the patient remained under anesthesia resting in the recovery room.

Kate glanced at her watch again and sighed.

The young woman returned with the child and took a seat in the chair next to Kate.

"Mrs. Meyers?" The young woman whispered.

"Yes..." Kate answered.

"I'm Gina. I come here a lot. I overheard the nurses talk about your husband yesterday." She continued whispering.

"What…what did you hear?" Kate gasped.

"He is unconscious, and on a ventilator. Apparently, he had a heart attack, and it weakened him so bad he had trouble breathing. Anyway, I overheard that they are going to do a test today to see if there is any brain activity. I am so sorry, ma'am."

Kate's eyes filled to the brim with tears that instantly spilled down her face. She inhaled deeply and Gina gripped her hand.

Kate couldn't talk. The tears flowed in a steady stream.

"Maybe they'll find brain activity, I am sorry this happened, but I had to tell you. You have a right to know."

"Thank you so much, Gina." Kate managed to mumble the words. "Do you happen to know what room he is in?"

"Yes, he is in Room 317."

Kate wiped her eyes and whispered. "They'll think I'm in the restroom, if they call my name, tell them I'll be right back."

Gina nodded.

Kate made her way down the hallway passing the restroom. It couldn't be seen from the information desk. She searched the room numbers on the doors. Taking a deep breath, she spotted Room 317. It had three notices taped to it stating various instructions to shift change nurses. Kate looked in both directions and saw no one in the hall. Relieved, she pushed the door open and entered.

Ethan lay sleeping in a mass of tubes and machines. Kate ran to his bed and stroked the side of his face with her hand.

"Oh, Ethan. It's me, Kate. Can you hear me, Ethan? I love you. I miss you. I've been praying for you."

Ethan never moved. Neither hand flinched. No eye movement. He lay perfectly still. Kate noticed how frail and helpless he appeared. She squeezed his hand and saw the bruises surrounding the I.V. on his other hand. She reached and gently rubbed her fingers across other bruises on his arm when suddenly, she felt strong hands grab her from behind.

A security guard stood and silently pulled her away from Ethan with all his strength. Kate stumbled and tried to break loose of his grip. He swayed back and forth and shoved her into the hallway. Clutching her arm tightly, he attempted to push her further away from Ethan's door.

"Let go of me." Kate demanded.

"You are not allowed in there." He spoke through clenched teeth.

Kate wiggled out of his grasp glaring at him. "You are about to be wrong. It's a matter of time, and..."

His voice grew raspy with rage as he interrupted her.

"Leave, or I will have you arrested, and I will press charges. So will the hospital."

"I don't have to leave. The waiting room is open to the public."

"Then get in there and stay there. Don't let me catch you near this room again." He huffed.

Kate darted down the hallway entering the waiting room with her hair in disarray, and visibly breathing loudly.

Gina ran to her.

"Come, sit down. Are you okay?"

"I am now. I got caught, but I don't care. I did get to see Ethan, and I thank you so much for that." She blurted and tried to slow her breathing to normal. "I guess I should explain what is going on."

"You don't have to."

"No, I want to. They insist on proof that I am married to Ethan. I had copies of my marriage license faxed to this hospital and to the police department here from Houston. They should have arrived by now. Until they receive them, they won't let me see him."

"That is incredible. I've never heard of having to show proof before seeing a spouse in a hospital."

"Well, Gina, that's what's going on."

The sharp clicking of high heels marching over the tile floor caught Kates's attention. Abruptly turning, she saw a tall woman in a business suit glaring as she approached.

"Are you Kate Meyers?" She asked sharply.

"Yes, I am."

"I know all about your kind. You are not welcome here."

"My kind? What do you mean?"

She glanced at the few remaining people in the waiting room. Raising both eyebrows, she eased closer to Kate and lowered her voice.

"It's common knowledge you protested at the high school for a more detailed sexual curriculum, and you are against corporal punishment. Every parent in town is upset with you. And you have the gall to wait for a marriage license to be faxed here? Why I can't believe anyone would consider marrying you." She held her head high and looked down at Kate.

"I don't know what you are talking about. What school? What curriculum? I haven't been to a school in years, and if I did, I would certainly hope they didn't give a more detailed sexual curriculum, and I hope they do have corporal punishment. A lot of students do want to learn, but some don't."

"Out. I've had enough. I won't fall for your faked innocence. Get out of my hospital."

"Your hospital? And you think you can talk down to me as if I were a child?"

"I am Dorothy Washington, the hospital administrator. I am instructing you to leave the premises." Her face reddened and a sheen of sweat broke out on her cheeks, chin, and forehead.

"And I am instructing you that the waiting room is a public place. Pardon me, but your arrogance isn't working. I will stay in the waiting room."

Dorothy Washington's eyes widened. "They were right. You are rude and have a trashy mouth." With that statement, she stomped off and nearly fell sideways in her high heels.

"You ought to be glad I'm not your employee; if I were, I'd report you. And you should treat others as you'd want to be treated."

"This is not Sunday School, Mrs. Meyers."

"No, it's not but you will answer to a higher authority for your actions, and that authority is God. Get ready, Mrs. Washington. The day of reckoning is coming for all of us."

"I don't have to listen to this."

Kate watched her disappear down a different hallway and uttered a quick prayer.

"Forgive me Lord. I couldn't bite my tongue. That is not the way to show her I'm a Christian, much less witness that Jesus Christ is my Savior and could be hers."

She turned to face Gina with

amazement. "How can she judge me like that? What in the world has she heard about me, and where did she get her information? I don't know anyone in this town."

"I don't know where she heard any of that. I do know most people who judge others are not addressing their own guilt."

"I totally agree." Kate wrinkled her nose. "Judgmental, superficial, and probably controlling; what an administrator. I may not have heard the last of her. If I need a witness, would you mind?"

"No, of course not, Mrs. Meyers."

"Kate. After what we've been through, call me Kate."

Gina nodded.

Digging through her purse, Kate pulled her phone out and hurried to make a call.

"Maria? Kate. Guess what? I sneaked in and saw Ethan." Kates's voice broke. "He looks awful, and he's unconscious. And I argued with the hospital security guard, and the administrator, but I'm okay. Tell Sal I've decided to move into the farmhouse anyway. At least I'll be closer to the hospital. I'll be back before dark to get my things and we can unload yours from the U-Haul then. I'll drive it back to the farmhouse." She paused and sounded more confident. "Yes, I'm sure. I'll see you later today. Alright. Bye."

Kate slipped the phone back into her purse. The restless night finally caught up with her. She yawned and slumped further down in her chair.

"Kate, why don't you close your eyes and rest awhile. I'll wake you if someone arrives with your marriage license."

"You'll still be here?"

"Oh, yes, I'll be here." Gina smiled from ear to ear.

"Okay, but only for a short time."

Gina nodded again as Kate drifted off to sleep. After playing patty cake with Elsa for an hour, Elsa soon tired and took her nap. Gina laid her beside Kate and went to the information desk.

"May I use the telephone?"

"Only if it's a local call." The woman snickered.

"It's to Jarmann Market, but I don't know the number."

The receptionist located the number, made the call and at the last minute, shoved the phone towards Gina.

Gina quickly snatched at the phone as it rang the market. "Hello? May I speak to Mrs. Schuhmacher? Thank you."

She waited and her face beamed as Mrs. Schuhmacher obviously answered.

"Hi, this is Gina. I missed seeing you earlier."

"We had an emergency, but it's been taken care of. Gina, I'm glad you called. You have the job. Can you start in the morning?"

"Yes. Thank you! I will see you

at nine o'clock."

Gina returned the phone and thanked the woman. Kate and Elsa were still sound asleep. She stepped lightly and sat in the chair next to her daughter.

Kate stirred in her chair and lifted her head.

"I think they call that a power nap." Unsteady, she attempted to rise, but rubbed her eyes instead. "What time is it?"

"Almost noon."

"You mean I slept that long?" Kate shook her head in amazement.

"I figured you needed to. Oh, and no news yet on your license, but I sure have some great news." Gina chatted.

"Oh? What is it?"

"I got hired at Jarmann Market. I called and I will start in the morning. They'll even help with my little daughter Elsa, at least until I find a permanent babysitter."

"Really? Well, helping with babysitting is unheard of. I'm happy for you if that's what you want."

"Oh yes, this is exactly what I want." Her eyes sparkled with joy as she spoke. "It's an answer to prayer. I couldn't have made it without my faith in God."

Kate glanced at her and smiled. "Let me share something with you. It's helped me when nothing else could. 'Come unto Me, all you who labor and are heavy laden, and I will give you rest. Take my yoke upon you, and learn you of Me; for I am meek and lowly in heart: and ye shall find rest unto your souls. For My yoke is easy, and My burden is light.' It's Matthew 11:28-30."

"Oh, I love it."

"I thought you would." Kate sputtered.

"It means a lot to me." A male replied.

Startled, Kate and Gina both jumped in their chairs and the policeman laughed.

"Excuse me, I should have interrupted you, but I wanted to listen to the scripture. I'm Daniel Leming."

"Kate Meyers … and this is my

friend, Gina…"

"Sehlke." Gina responded. "Gina Sehlke."

He nodded at both of them and approached Kate.

"Ma'am, your fax came in at the police station. I have a copy of your marriage license." He handed it to her, and she shook her head.

"Thank you, Mr. Leming, and thank You Lord Jesus! I can legally see my husband now."

"Legally?" Daniel Leming inquired.

"It's a long story." Kate said as she dashed to the information desk. "Here is my license. Make a copy. I'm going to Room 317." Kate left without waiting for a reply.

The receptionist grabbed the page and inserted it into the copy machine. As soon as the machine spit out a copy, Gina ran and stood with her hand extended.

"I'll take the original."

The police officer stood beside Gina and smiled. She received the original with no problem. They sat and waited as Kate went alone to visit her husband.

"I'm surprised the security guard and the administrator haven't tried to stop Kate again. They wouldn't let her see him without proof she is actually his wife. She had a fax sent to this hospital and the police station here."

"Well, we received our copy thirty minutes ago. The hospital should have had theirs about the same time."

"The administrator breezed by here a while ago trying to get Kate to leave. Surely, she hadn't received the fax earlier. I mean, Kates's husband is unconscious and on a ventilator. You'd think that the hospital would have contacted her as soon as they knew she could visit him."

"Yes, ma'am, you would think so. I don't understand why they wouldn't, but it appears she would still be sitting in this waiting room if I hadn't brought ours over. Makes you wonder why, doesn't it?"

"Yes, it does."

Kate emerged from the adjoining hallway veering towards them.

Her eyes were red-rimmed but this time they were dry.

Kates trembled as she tried to talk. "He is too pale. Looks so worn out." She glanced at the police officer. "Thanks again for all your help."

He stood and nodded while handing her his card. "If I can be of service, give me a call."

He left the hospital as Kate and Gina returned to their chairs. Elsa still slept soundly.

"I can't do anything for Ethan. If I stayed in his room, I'm afraid I'd drift off to sleep and fall on him or fall into the machine. It would be better for both of us if I returned in the morning. I'm going home, Gina. I want to hear all about your new job tomorrow, maybe I can come over to see you after you get off work? Where do you live?"

"Kate, I'll be here." Gina spoke in a hushed tone.

"Who is it you are seeing here?"

"Kate…no one knows this, but…I live here. I stay in the bathroom here at night, and pretend I visit a patient during the day and…"

Kate stopped her in mid-sentence.

"And now you'll stay with me. Get Elsa, and let's go home. I'll see to it that you get to work on time."

"Kate, you don't know me that well."

"No, I don't. I may not know

about you, but I know your heart."

Gina, visibly shaken, pulled her sleeping daughter from the chair. Her voice cracked with emotion. "We're going home, Elsa."

The little girl opened and closed her eyes, returning to blissful sleep.

Taking a deep breath and looking at Kate, Gina silently mouthed the words, "thank you."

Chapter Twenty-One

Douglas Futrell parked his rented car and removed a piece of lint from his jacket as he exited the vehicle. He entered the attorney's office wearing a light grey three-piece suit with a solid rust-brown tie and a medium brown Stetson Chatham Fedora hat cocked gently to one side. A hint of Boss cologne lingered about his being. With his manicured hands, he handed the secretary a card bearing his name and tipped his hat with the other.

Quite handsome in a rugged way, he hid his true self behind the clothes a gentleman would wear. He clearly enjoyed the impression he made and purposely arrived early for the appointment.

Mesmerized, the secretary flashed him a wide smile and obviously forgot that she had been typing.

Leaning forward, she shook her head and appeared coy while allowing her long, dark brown hair to fall over her desk.

"Hello. I'm Douglas Futrell." He snickered. "I have an eleven-thirty appointment with Mr. Bailey."

"Uh, hello. Please have a seat, Mr. Futrell. I'll tell Mr. Bailey you are here." She quickly straightened her posture and blushed.

Douglas narrowed his eyes at her and nodded as he selected a chair.

She informed her employer of

Douglas's arrival.

Pulling a magazine from the wall rack, he settled in the chair and immersed himself in turning pages at random.

Twice he caught her gaze lingering in his direction and chose to ignore her. He unbuttoned his suit jacket, exposing the tight vest and the massiveness of his bulging chest. Had he been wearing a tank top; he would have flexed his muscles at her at this time. A well-played game to Douglas, he loved every minute of it.

"Mr. Bailey's ready for you. You may go in now."

"Thank you, ma'am."

Douglas strolled across the room as the attorney opened the door.

"Douglas Futrell. Nice to meet you. Come in."

He escorted the potential client into his office and shut the door.

"How'd we do?" Douglas asked.

"She fell for it. I'm sure Octavia thinks you are simply a client. Sit down." Richard Bailey motioned to a chair in front of his desk.

Douglas sprawled into the brown leather, wing-back chair and loosened his tie.

"Octavia?"

"Octavia Leigh, my new secretary. She's only eighteen, and this is her first job. How naïve can one be? And I'll point out the importance of you only dating Judy. Octavia is way too young for you."

"Point taken."

"Do you have the money? Any trouble getting it?" The attorney inquired.

"No. They behaved during their so-called emergency." Douglas laughed. "I told them if it got out they were robbed, I'd keep returning until they were forced to close."

"I knew you could handle it. Well done, my friend."

Douglas lazily stood and approached the desk. Taking a wad of bills from both of his front pants pockets; he counted out one hundred dollars to each stack. Carefully overlaying each pile, he added one-hundred-dollar bills into stacks of thousands.

Lifting his eyes at Richard Bailey when he finished, he spoke with a firm voice. "For services to be rendered."

"Piece of cake." Richard stated. "How much did you get me?"

"I already counted it. You count it now."

The attorney counted and recounted the stacks of money three times.

"Fifteen thousand."

Douglas took a long pause before responding. "Exactly what I came up with. The owners claimed that part of their annual insurance payment got mixed up with their weekly income."

"Well, I bet fifteen thousand won't ever sit in their safe again." Richard laughed.

"Nope." Douglas joined in the laughter.

"So, we need to get started right away. Ethan Meyers isn't going to be around much longer. I'll file an affidavit stating you are his only living next of kin and plead the court will hand over a clear title of the property."

"Good, the sooner the better. Ethan's wife received her marriage license copy today. Dorothy Washington talked to Judy about that and their encounter. She also told Judy they are testing him for any brain activity tomorrow."

Douglas raised an eyebrow.

Richard nodded. "Judy Harris certainly made life difficult for Kate. She did great with the school's opinions. Got the whole town against both of them. Some people think he did kill his other wife, and no one believes their marriage license is authentic. Kate won't have a leg to stand on in court."

"Not in this town." Douglas predicted. "That reminds me, I'm on my way to supposedly run into Judy where she works. We planned it well. The townspeople will think two long-lost school chums met today after years apart. Then we'll date, go out to local restaurants…be squeaky clean. They will have no problem in court believing her when it comes to my reputation. And you and I both know this will end up in court."

"Oh yes, it certainly will. And I need to cut our meeting short, I've got papers for Octavia to notarize before this afternoon's court session."

"I have to run, too." Douglas tipped his hat at the attorney.

"You sly dog." He chuckled as Douglas went out the door.

He walked past the secretary's desk and winked at her as he turned to leave.

Her eyes widened and she stared incredibly at him.

He hurried to the car and called Judy.

"I'm on my way."

"I can't wait to finally see you again." She cooed on the phone.

"I bet you can't." He muttered.

"What? What did you say?"

"I said I bet you can." He spoke with light sarcasm.

She chuckled. "See you soon."

Pushing his foot down hard on the gas pedal, the rental car sped off to the Crockett Co-Op. He arrived in minutes, and once again entered an office looking like a male magazine model.

The manager of the billing department glanced up from her desk.

"May I help you, sir?"

"Yes ma'am. I'm trying to find Judy Harris. Does she still work here?"

All heads turned in his direction from each work cubicle in the 20 x 20 room.

"Yes, she does. Is this work-related, or an emergency?"

"It is an emergency to me, but it'll be a surprise to her. I haven't seen Judy since we were in school together...a few years ago." He gave her his shy, half-grin.

"Oh, well." She fluttered about and came out of her cubicle. "It is almost lunchtime anyway. I don't see any harm in getting her." She seemed to purr as she gazed at him.

Texting Judy on her phone, she glanced again at the stranger.

"And you are?"

"Forgive me for not introducing myself, ma'am. I'm Douglas Futrell. I'm excited beyond all imagination."

Judy appeared in the room at that moment. Placing her hand over her mouth, she stopped in her tracks.

"It can't be. Oh my, is it really you, Douglas? After all these years…"

She ran to him and received a huge bear hug. They appeared to wipe their eyes, but in reality, Douglas roughly touched the corners of their dry eyes, and they blinked rapidly until their eyes did water. It worked enough for Judy's co-workers to be emotional, and their eyes had genuine tears.

"Everyone, this is Douglas

Futrell. I can't believe it's really him. We went to school together in our younger years."

"Younger years? Why Judy, you look amazing. May I have the pleasure of taking you to lunch?"

"Lunch? Yes, I'd love it. Do you remember Sissy Weekly? She owns the Blue Frog Restaurant downtown and serves the best home cooked daily specials you'll find anywhere."

"Sissy Weekly? The name sounds familiar. Let's eat there."

He put his arm across Judy's shoulders and escorted her to the door.

"I promise to have her back in an hour." He tipped his hat to the manager, and they escaped the prying eyes.

Climbing into the car, they burst out laughing.

"Lady, we did great."

"We did, didn't we?"

"So, Judy, we eat at the Blue Frog, and I'll try to eat everything on my plate. Good impressions go a long way."

"Don't overdo it."

"I won't."

They arrived and strolled inside, casually looking for an empty table in the packed restaurant.

"Judy? Over here." A woman motioned towards a corner table.

They maneuvered through the groups of customers, many recently arriving as they did.

Picking up on bits of conversation, they walked past crowded tables. Several had five chairs for a table seating four. The woman handed each of them an opened menu as they eased into a chair.

Douglas nodded at Judy to order while he studied the selections.

"I'll have the chicken fried steak with seasoned green beans, mashed potatoes, and brown gravy, and a slice of fresh strawberry pie with whipped cream on top."

Douglas gulped. "Sounds delicious. I'll have the same thing."

"You won't be disappointed."

Judy smiled.

"And to drink?" The woman paused as she turned to leave the table.

"Iced tea, unsweetened." Douglas answered.

"A glass of one-third sweetened lemonade, and two-thirds unsweetened tea. I think you call it an 'Arnold Palmer'. It's the most refreshing cold drink I've found." Judy glanced at the woman. "With lots of ice, please."

"No problem." She took off and disappeared among the customers.

"Judy, how are you?"

Douglas and Judy turned in the direction of the greeting and found themselves looking at a group of four couples.

"I'm fine. It's always good to see old friends. Let me introduce you to Douglas Futrell. Douglas, this is Bob and Frances Polk, Robert and Gloria McCluthens, Bobbie and Amy Henderson, and Judd and Susan Warren."

"Nice to meet you." Some spoke together, and others simply nodded.

"This is the first time we've seen each other since our school years. Douglas surprised me a while ago at my office." Judy drawled.

Douglas grinned. "I guess you could say this lunch is our first date."

"Well, you two enjoy your time together. We'll catch up with you later." They glanced at Judy with raised eyebrows and smiled. A waiter ushered them off to a large table.

"I'm glad Richard changed your last name to Futrell…you're the only Futrell in the county," Judy whispered.

"And no one knows what school we attended. Talk about perfect timing." Douglas displayed a wide grin.

A waiter brought their food and hurried off.

Douglas cut into his chicken fried steak and took a bite. "This is really good, Judy. We'll have to come here again."

"We will, but remember, I have to be back at work in less than an hour."

"You will be. Don't worry."

"Oh, that reminds me. Douglas, did you like the clothes I bought for you?"

"Yes. Excellent purchases."

"Well, I couldn't figure out why you wanted the police uniform."

"It has to do with my being in prison." He laughed. "I wanted to wear it and pretend."

Douglas reached for his glass of tea when his phone rang. He frowned and glanced at Judy.

"Who in the world?"

She grimaced and shook her head.

"Hello?"

"Hey, it's me, Richard. Have Judy talk to her hospital contacts and find out what Ethan Meyers' blood type is."

"Okay. Consider it done."

"Oh, if you don't know what yours is, give blood somewhere and Douglas, they'll tell you what your blood type is."

"Are you sure they will tell you?"

"No, I'm not, but we have to know, and it has to be discrete. You're not going to faint from giving blood, are you?"

"No, Richard, but there has to be another way. I mean, what if I give blood and no-one informs me what my blood type is?"

"Then you will have helped someone in the community. I think you have to pay a laboratory to find out. That's why I thought about giving blood. At least it's free. Some places even give you a free t-shirt."

"That's exactly what I need, Richard, a free t-shirt."

"Don't knock it. Hopefully, you and Ethan have the same blood type. If not, I'll come up with another angle. Douglas, I'll figure it out."

"Okay, I'll have my blood drawn as soon as I return Judy to the Co-Op."

Richard ended the call and buzzed his secretary.

"Octavia, you can leave for lunch. I've got papers for you to notarize when you return. I'll put them on your desk as I lock up to go to lunch."

Focused on typing a letter, she jumped at the sound of his voice. Still jittery, she sprang from her chair and quickly answered him on the intercom.

"Thank you, I'll leave now." Grabbing her purse and car keys, she took off.

Richard rushed to set the papers on her desk, and accidentally knocked a small artificial plant off. It lay on the floor with leaves in disarray.

Groaning, he snatched it up and placed it near the intercom on her desk.

He gasped.

The intercom is on...the button is down...did I accidentally press the button turning it on...or did she leave it on? Surely not. Surely, she turned it off earlier…maybe she simply turned it on when I called about lunch...how long has it been on? I have to buy new phones that light up the button when the intercom is on…

He flinched as he stared at the intercom.

Am I getting paranoid?

Chapter Twenty-Two

Side by side, Kate, Gina, and Elsa left the hospital and entered the parking lot. Not a breeze blew, nor were any birds present. No familiar chirping. It seemed as if time stood still, and they were walking through it. No train noise, no car traffic, no one walking anywhere, nothing.

Kate frowned at Gina.

"Something doesn't feel right. I know I said you're going home with me, and you are, but I think I need to tell the police I'm moving back to the farmhouse."

She unlocked the car, and they climbed in. Glancing at Gina, she continued.

"I'll call the police officer, Daniel Leming. He seemed nice. He can tell a detective I'm moving in today."

"I don't understand. Why do you have to tell them you're moving in?"

"Someone caused some damage when we first arrived from Houston, but nothing else has happened since. We'll be okay, though."

"Are you sure?"

"Yes." She retrieved the card Daniel Leming had given her with his phone number and called him.

"Hello, Mr. Leming?"

"Yes."

"This is Kate Meyers. We met earlier at the hospital. You brought me a copy of my marriage license."

"Yes, ma'am. What can I do for you?"

"Could you inform a detective there that I'm moving into the farmhouse? I assume a detective is in charge of our case as the farmhouse is under surveillance. Two deputies came to the farmhouse to see the damage someone made when we first arrived from Houston. Their names are Ira Pascal and Caleb Davis. They are aware of what happened at that time. Anyway, nothing else has happened out there, so I'm going to move in."

"I will check into it and get back

to you. Your number is on my caller I.D. I'll call when I know something."

"Thank you. I'm moving now, so if you can't get me, I probably won't be able to get a signal. You know how some cell phones are."

"I'll get in touch."

"Thank you."

Kate ended the call and turned to Gina.

"I feel better now. Ready for a brand-new start?"

Gina closed her eyes and sighed. "Oh, yes. That's all I can think about."

"We'll go to Sal and Maria's and get my things there. Then help them unload their belongings from the U-Haul trailer, so I can bring the trailer with us. We'll have to unload it today because you start your job tomorrow, and I can turn the U-Haul trailer in after that, and then go see Ethan…" Kate hesitated and grinned at Gina.

"Talk about busy, we are jumping into it with both feet, and we haven't thought about lunch yet."

Gina laughed. "Lunch? What is that? Can we work it in?"

"Of course, we can. Will fried chicken work? Or hamburgers? What about Elsa? What will she eat?"

"Elsa will eat whatever you put in front of her. Either one you mentioned will be a treat, believe me. And I will make this up to you." Gina bounced her daughter on her lap.

Kate glanced at the two passengers. "We have to get a car seat for her today, too. Let's eat and go shopping before going to Sal and Maria's."

"Sounds great to me." Gina nodded.

They ordered lunch at a local fast-food restaurant. The fried chicken aroma wafted through the air and smelled better than any other fried chicken one could imagine. Taking their time, they ate in the car savoring the taste of crunchy battered moist chicken with mashed potatoes and gravy, and hot, homemade yeast rolls. Three and a half hours later, and after checking out the baby department in four stores; they purchased the perfect car seat and even had it installed.

Kate, Gina, and Elsa arrived at Sal and Maria's shortly after five o'clock. Kate noticed the U-Haul had been moved.

Exiting the Chevy, Kate waited for Gina to remove her daughter from the car seat. Maria and Sal came rushing out, hugging Kate as she stood by the car.

"We have a surprise for you, lady." They grinned.

Kate gave them a puzzled expression with a slight smile.

"You do? What can it be?"

Sal waved his arms over his head. "Come on, come on, we'll show you." They marched to the U-Haul, and he opened the back door.

Kate gasped. "It's half empty. All I see are mine and Ethans things." She turned to gaze at them with an open mouth.

"We unloaded our stuff after you called. Oh, and you don't have to worry about the condition of the farmhouse. Monroe let us borrow some workers and cleaning supplies. It's all been taken care of. Even the shattered glass in the kitchen is gone. Everything is nice and clean." Sal beamed.

"We did have to throw the kitchen curtains away, too many glass particles. You can get new ones later." Maria stated.

Tears sprang in Kate's eyes and fell down her cheeks. She sobbed out loud and hugged both Sal and

Maria tightly.

"Thank you. Thank you. Thank you." She whispered.

Their eyes also watered as emotions overwhelmed each of them.

"We help each other." Sal managed to say.

"And we sure have." Kate's voice shook as she broke apart from them. She wiped her tears and tried to smile.

"I forgot to introduce you to Gina and her daughter, Elsa. She helped me see Ethan at the hospital...and needs a place to stay...so I'm..."

Sal interrupted her. "So, you're taking them home with you."

"Yes, I am."

"Exactly like she brought us up here from Houston." He glanced at Gina. "She is a good person. You will find that out." He and Maria gave each other a knowing grin.

"I am finding it out, and I will repay her for her kindness somehow." Gina shook her head.

"Kate, I took the liberty to pack your things in your bedroom. It's in a box in the U-Haul." Maria walked to the trailer, and she pointed to a certain box apart from the others.

"Thanks, Maria, that will save time. I'm anxious to get settled and return to check on Ethan."

"I can guide you to the trailer hitch if you want to back up now." Sal said.

"Yes, we need to get going."

Kate and her passengers climbed into the car and Kate backed into position. Sal attached the trailer, and Kate lowered her window.

"Thanks again. Love you guys."

"We love you too and call us if we can help with anything. This place worked out great for us. I love my job, and the kids love it here." Sal added.

Kate slowly drove out of their parking lot when Maria came running.

"Wait. You forgot Rufus."

"Oh my gosh, I did. Poor little dog."

Sal took off in a dash and hurried back with the dog and a bag of dog food.

"Where's his leash? And you forgot his bed and his toys…" Maris scowled.

"Hey, I'm the one who forgot the entire dog." Kate laughed.

They soon had Rufus in the car. He wiggled with excitement at seeing Kate. He jumped into her lap and licked her chin as Maria put his stuff on the floorboard in the back seat. Elsa squealed at the happy dog who twisted around in Kate's lap.

"We're going to stop at the market on our way to the farmhouse. That ought to be exciting." Kate waved by to the couple, and they left.

"They seemed like nice people, caring." Gina said.

"They are. We evacuated from Hurricane Harvey together." Kate sighed. "Their journey ends and ours begins." She smiled.

"I hope ours ends as well as theirs." Gina spoke wistfully.

"Oh, it will, Gina. I believe in the power of prayer."

"Me too."

Kate relaxed her posture and glanced at Gina. "Want to get groceries where you'll soon be working?"

"Sure, I'd like that."

"Okay, coming right up."

Chapter Twenty-Three

Douglas returned home before Judy got off of work. Unbuttoning his suit jacket, he ran his hand across the leather belt and holster hidden under it. Scanning the living room, he thumbed the strap over the weapon's trigger and released the metal snap. He pulled the gun from the holster and glanced at it.

Any gun was highly illegal for him to have, yet easy to obtain. A prison buddy told him the name of a local drug dealer who'd get him a long barrel 357 Magnum for the right money. And he still had money. The attorney didn't receive all of what he'd robbed, nor did the drug dealer.

He raised the end of the couch and tore material off the bottom. Setting it back on the floor, he carefully wiped the gun with a napkin from his pocket and placed the gun under the couch. He laid it flat on a wooden corner. Douglas stuffed the ripped cloth around it and kicked at the couch. The gun remained hidden and secure.

He wiped the box of ammunition for it with the same napkin and set it behind several books piled high on a shelf. Digging into his pocket, he withdrew small zip-lock bags of a white powdery substance, and a package bulging with pills. These he slipped behind another stack of books in the middle of the shelf.

And that's my protection for the new business venture…mine and Richard's meth lab…

He surveyed the hiding places with a pleased expression.

Judy never reads, and seldom comes in this room. Her television is in her bedroom as is her computer...and me. He chuckled.

His gaze wandered across the room taking in random objects Judy had on other shelves. Glass figurines, pictures of people he didn't recognize, and a few antique oil lamps. Another shelf had a wicker basket full of pinecone potpourri with a faint hint of cinnamon.

She probably sprinkles it with essential oils...man, I can't take this much longer...makes me think of the old saying, 'a place for everything and' ...and ...heck, I don't remember. I am sick of being in this place and sick of being with Judy...but I need her...for now…

Judy opened the door and her merry voice sailed through the house. "Hey, I'm home. Knock, knock, anyone here?"

Douglas cringed, then immediately plastered a phony smile on his hardened face.

"Coming."

He met her in the hallway and planted a kiss on her forehead. "Welcome home."

"And I like that welcome." She gazed up at him and her legs wobbled.

Douglas leaned back against the wall, seemingly at ease and in control.

"How about a dinner date?"

Her eyes sparkled. "I'd love it. Let me change out of these clothes and freshen my make-up. I'll hurry." She raced off before he could reply.

He entered the kitchen and sat in a chair, tapping his foot against the tiled floor. Finally, he crossed and uncrossed his legs and glanced at the wall clock. Five minutes crawled by. He stood and paced aimlessly appearing lost in thought.

Judy spotted him and entered the kitchen wearing tight blue jeans, boots, and a flowing blouse made of silk.

Douglas stopped pacing and looked at her in amazement.

"Well, hello Judy." He whistled.

She promptly displayed satisfied, catlike stretches and approached him.

"Hello to you too."

He backed away from her and sounded exasperated. "Now I have to change clothes. I can't wear a suit when you're in jeans."

"Well go change. Hurry." She playfully touched his shoulder and shoved him forward.

With his back to her, she missed the cold expression of annoyance that flashed across his face. Leaving the kitchen, he involuntarily shivered.

Changing into jeans and a lightweight pullover sweater didn't take long. Hanging the three-piece suit so it wouldn't wrinkle is what took time. After he hung it in the closet, he stuck his feet into his own boots and rinsed his mouth with Colgate mouthwash in the bathroom. A quick mist of body spray, and he hastened back to Judy.

He draped his arm across her waist and escorted her to the door. "Ready?"

"Ready."

"You choose. Where do you want to eat?"

"No. What about you, Douglas? What do you like?"

"Don't worry about me. This is your night."

"Okay, then …how about Mexican food?"

"Love it."

She locked the front door as they left the house, and they strolled side by side to the car. Out of habit, she climbed behind the wheel. He glanced at her with a slight smile and slipped into the passenger's side of the front seat.

"Oh, I'm not thinking." She gushed. "Do you want to drive?"

"I'm good. Let's go."

They arrived at Pancho Villa's Cantina in Crockett to discover it was standing room only. Douglas gave his name to the hostess, Vickie Jones, who promised the wait would only be a few minutes.

Locals instantly surrounded Judy. Everyone talked about Douglas offering a community garden and congratulated him on standing up for his rights.

He nodded and smiled and grabbed Judy tightly by her arm when Vickie called them to follow her. Their small table sat in a corner with barely enough room to sit much less eat. Judy opened a menu and focused on it. Vickie left promising their waitress would take their order soon. Douglas leaned forward and glared at Judy.

"What have you done?"

"What are you talking about?"

"You know exactly what I'm referring to. A community garden at the farmhouse? And me standing up for my rights? Judy, are you out of your mind? No one is supposed to know I'm after Ethan Meyers' property."

"I simply wanted more people

on your side…and they are. Douglas, if you stop and think about it, offering land for a community garden is unheard of. It's why they admire you for it. Don't get mad at it. I had your best interests at heart." She slumped in her chair and hung her head.

He reached across the table and squeezed her hand. "It's okay. You meant well. I'll have to make the best of it. I'll figure it out."

The waitress arrived and took their order. Another waitress brought a basket of tortilla chips with each a small bowl of red salsa and a green one to sample. Drinks were served. Douglas and Judy munched hungrily without further conversation. Their food arrived sizzling loudly, and Judy asked for more napkins.

The steam from their plates of beef fajitas rose enticingly. Douglas inhaled deeply as the aroma hit their nostrils.

"Umm. Glad we came here. A wise choice, Judy."

"Thanks. It does smell yummy. Does that mean we're still friends?" She tried to smile, and her chin trembled.

"Judy, I'm sorry about getting angry. Of course, we're still friends. And I'd like for us to soon be more than friends." He stammered.

A waiter dropped off the extra napkins as he dashed by. Judy watched him leave and quickly gave Douglas her full attention.

"You don't know how hard I try to please you, and..." She blushed as he interrupted her.

"Judy, I admire you and your efforts. I don't know anyone else that would help me as you have. I do thank you. Now, let's eat before the food gets cold."

She straightened her back and sat with perfect posture as she raised her head making eye contact with him. "Don't get onto me for trying to help you, then. It's a tough pill to swallow."

He grimaced and squeezed her hand again.

They ate with pleasant chit-chat during the remainder of the meal. Their moment of confrontation ended.

Driving home, she talked constantly about everyone she'd seen at the restaurant. She either put someone up on an unearned pedestal or put another down for something she'd been obviously jealous of. She shared secrets about one of them as he quietly patted his foot on the floorboard.

"I need to stop for gas, we're nearly empty. You look so comfortable sprawled over there, I'll pump the gas." She sputtered and pulled into a gas station.

"Thanks. I need to make a call anyway."

She stopped at the pump and dug through her purse for her gas card. Grabbing it, she bounced out of the car and inserted her card after selecting the grade of gas she used. Douglas pulled his phone from his pocket and quickly punched in a set of numbers. The phone rang on the other end. A gruff voice answered.

"Hello?"

"Richard?"

"Yes, who is this?"

"It's me, Douglas. Listen, Judy spread it all over town about my wanting the Meyers property, among other stuff."

"She has to spread the wrong kind of gossip, doesn't she?"

"Yeah, afraid so, Richard. I told her to spread gossip about Ethan and Kate. I can't believe she started spreading gossip about me."

"Well, we can't have her talking about anything else we do, or I should say …going to do. Douglas, the meth lab is happening, and plans are all made. My contacts are ready."

"I have contacts too, Richard. They agree the Meyers farmhouse is a perfect location. Isolated."

"And the small airport fifteen miles away is never checked for anything. Great distribution resource."

"Exactly." Douglas snapped.

"Kate will be served the papers tomorrow suing her for the property. Did you get your bloodwork done?"

"No, Richard. I'll go to another town and have it done tomorrow. And I still have to ask Judy to find out what Ethan's blood type is."

"I'll find another way to get Ethan's blood type, and Douglas?"

"Yes?"

"Judy has got to go. Understand?"

"I understand."

Chapter Twenty-Four

Kate parked across the back of the parking lot to accommodate the U-Haul trailer. Without realizing it, she made quite an impressive public display. Circling twice before she chose the back of the lot, everyone stopped and watched her carefully driving past their parked vehicles. It caught the attention of the Schuhmacher twins.

She and her passengers exited the Chevy Suburban and approached the store's entrance. Gina held little Elsa's hand letting her walk at her own pace. At the door, a customer leaving exchanged a glance with Kate.

"You sure have a big load to pull, lady. I'm glad it's you and not me." The woman chuckled and left the store. Kate and Gina walked in, and Kate grabbed a bascart. Gina looked at her daughter and laughed. Elsa was standing wide-eyed looking at all the food items.

"Too much temptation, Elsa. You'd get into everything." She reached for her daughter and carried her. Turning, she nearly ran into one of the Schuhmacher twins.

"Karl, hi, or are you, Kurt?"

"It's me Karl. Nice to see you, Gina."

"You too. Oh, and this is my friend, Kate. I live with her."

Kate stopped rolling the bascart. "Good to meet you, Karl. Gina told me she starts working here tomorrow."

"Yes, we're happy to have her. It's good to meet you also, and I have to commend you on your driving skills, I am impressed. That is a long U-Haul trailer."

"Thank you. We have to unload it as soon as we're through here. It's only half full though. I'd better finish getting the groceries. You two go on and visit." Kate nodded and hastened off.

"Are you moving somewhere?"

"We are moving in. It's a long story, Karl. The place we're going to is Kate and her husband's farmhouse. He's in the hospital, and…"

"In the hospital? Well, Gina, I can't let you ladies leave here without having someone to unload the U-Haul for you. I'll get my brother, and we'll follow you to this farmhouse."

"Thank you, Karl. I can't turn down that offer. Kate will appreciate it also. She'll be happy when I tell her we have help."

"Go ahead. I'll get Kurt. Don't leave without us now."

"We won't."

Gina finally found her friend roaming the aisles with a full bascart of groceries and supplies. "Kate, there you are. Have I got good news for you."

"I'm ready for good news, Gina. What is it?"

Raising her eyebrows, Gina whispered in hushed, excitable tones, "Karl and his brother, Kurt, are going to unload the U-Haul for us."

"Thank You Lord Jesus!" Kate's face beamed with a wide smile. "I'm done here. Let's hurry and check out."

Kate whirled the bascart around and darted to the check-out counter near the store's entrance. As soon as her items were bagged, she paid and went to the door to wait on the twins. They had changed from their dress clothes and arrived in old blue jeans and stained work shirts.

Gina made introductions and the twins helped load the groceries in the back of the Suburban. Kate gave them directions in case too many cars got between them.

"Thanks again for your help." Kate sang out as they rolled out of the parking lot. With traffic being light, the Schuhmacher's followed in their truck at a decent distance.

Kate drove while Gina sat in the front passenger seat holding Rufus. Elsa, in the car seat, had the entire back seat to herself. She enjoyed kicking her legs and looking out the window.

"Which one of the twins is driving?" Kate squinted at Gina.

"I don't know." Gina laughed.

"Well, from the way the first one looked at you, I'd say you better find out."

Gina sighed with a playful grin. "Karl. He is the first one. Hmm." Her eyes sparkled as words rushed out excitedly. "Maybe he can tell me what color shirt he's wearing or something, while I'm working with both of them." She glanced out the window, and a smile remained on her beaming face.

Kate observed her embarrassed friend with fondness and left Gina alone with her thoughts of Karl. Kate drove another fifteen minutes before exiting from the highway. The main road appeared peaceful, and Kate could be silent no longer.

"Hearing the crunch of this gravel road under the car's wheels is going to be part of our routine. It's as calming as a country breeze in the springtime." Kate jabbered visibly relaxed and gazed ahead at the road.

As Kate drove over the last curve, and the farmhouse came into view, she turned to Gina. "We're home."

The pleasant look on Kates's face disappeared the instant she looked at Gina.

Wide-eyed, Gina's face paled as she stared at the farmhouse and gasped.

In a pleading tone, she whispered. "I'm so sorry. I am so sorry Kate." Gina burst out sobbing loudly, and Rufus started barking. Kate took her foot off the gas.

"What? What is it?"

"Keep driving. I…I don't want the twins to know, not yet. Not now." Gina flashed a bewildered look at Kate. "Please."

Elsa took one look at her mother crying, and she wailed even louder.

"It's okay, Elsa, Mama feels

better." She reached into the car seat and patted her. Elsa stopped crying and patted her mama's arm.

Kate barely accelerated. "Gina, what's wrong?"

"I didn't always stay at the hospital. I had been homeless for a while. At one time, I camped out behind this house."

Kate stopped the car and whirled about in the front seat facing Gina. "You camped here? The tent, the canned food?"

"Yes. Elsa and I were fine until this guy Douglas showed up. I had to escape in the middle of the night to get away from him. Such an ugly man inside and out." Gina's shoulders shook with repressed sobs. "I don't know how long he stayed. I never came back." Her posture crumpled as she spoke. With her head hanging down, she raised her eyes up to meet Kate's eyes. "Please forgive me."

"Gina, you had a bad experience here. Let's talk about it later. You haven't done anything to be forgiven for." Kate leaned over and hugged Gina on her shoulders.

"Now, let's get moved into the farmhouse." Kate slowly accelerated and the car eased down the road. She waved to the twins in their truck.

"Wipe your tears. We are starting over."

"Thank you." Gina managed a smile. "I think I have butterflies in my stomach. Can you believe it? At my age?"

"Your age? What are you, twenty?"

"I'm twenty-one."

"Well, I'm not twenty-one, and I have butterflies too." Kate's voice rose as she spoke. "And this excitement is overwhelming." Her eyes watered. "We are actually here and we're moving in."

Gina nodded and choked back a sob.

Kate pulled the car as close to the front porch as possible.

"New beginnings." Kate stated as she stopped the car.

"Yes, new beginnings. I can't wait." Gina declared firmly.

Kate and Gina rushed out and the brothers weren't far behind. The twins soon walked to the back of the trailer and waited for Kate to unlock it.

"I thought you two were backing out when you stopped the car. Everything alright?" One of the twins asked.

Kate smiled. "Just a little pep talk. It's all good."

"Pep talks are best when they pop up unexpectedly."

"Which one of you just said that?" Gina teased.

"I did, it came from me, Karl. Those words of wisdom came from me."

"No, me, Kurt. I am full of words of wisdom."

Both of the twins quickly looked at each other and laughed.

"We couldn't resist. Anyway, I'm Karl with the blue shirt on, and Kurt is wearing the green shirt."

"Thanks. Now I know who I'm talking to." Gina said as she sat Elsa on the porch.

"Anytime." Karl replied. He and his brother climbed inside the trailer glancing at the contents. Within an hour, they had the trailer unloaded. Boxes were all inside the house. What furniture the Meyers brought from Houston now had a home in various rooms of the farmhouse.

"Can we help with anything else?" Kurt asked as they walked to their truck.

"No, you have both been great." Kate smiled. "Thanks again."

"We'd still be unloading if it hadn't been for you two." Gina added.

"Our pleasure. Glad to help." The twins called out. "See you in the morning, Gina."

"I'll be there. Please wear different colored shirts."

"No problem."

Kate and Gina watched the truck disappear on the winding gravel road.

"We did it!" Kate yelled.

Gina whooped loudly. "Yes ma'am, we did!"

"Hey, it's not too late. Let's return the U-Haul trailer and be done with it."

"Sounds good to me."

They left Rufus in the house, locked it, and Gina slowly placed Elsa in her car seat.

"You know something, Kate?"

"What?"

"This will be a great time to finish our talk when you stopped the car earlier."

"If you're up to it, Gina. We could wait."

"No, I want to get things out in the open. I'll feel better, and you won't have to wonder about it."

Kate smiled at her as they entered the car.

"Okay." Kate spoke in a caring tone as she pulled out of the front yard. Gina shifted her weight and got comfortable in the front seat.

"I used to be happily married. Loved to cook, and I enjoyed a clean house. My husband and I attended church. We did everything together. Laughed a lot. Both of us were so in love with each other. Always did little things for each other. A happy marriage. Nothing about self. Discussed everything. We put God first, then each other. Prayed for God's will in our lives and had it. Then we had Elsa. Things were greater than you could imagine. He served in the Army. I worked for a total of four years for the Ammerman & Moseley CPA firm in Ft. Leavenworth, Kansas. That's where my husband died. He had a massive heart attack. After he died, I left. I looked for a place to settle but ended up homeless. I've worked odd jobs and stayed in shelters. And I don't recommend anyone camping out behind a vacant house, but we had peace and quiet." Her voice suddenly took on a harsh tone. "That is until Douglas showed up. He had long unkempt matted hair and an enormous bushy beard. Nasty man. Vulgar language. Controlling. Ordered me around. Anyway, I never let him touch me, but day and night I remained afraid he'd try to grab me. I had to sneak off in the middle of the night with Elsa to get away from him. I've been staying at the hospital ever since." Gina shrugged her shoulders.

"Thank God Douglas didn't hurt you. Gina, do you realize the extent of danger you were in? He could have sold you as a sex slave to someone or killed you. No one knew where you were, and no one knew to report your absence. It's a miracle you are alive, and you still have your daughter. He could have kidnapped her and sold her." Kate shuttered as she spoke.

"I realize it now, and thank God, we met each other at the hospital." Gina looked straight at Kate. "I've experienced scary, but important lessons this year by not doing His will. Now, I always pray for God's guidance and His will. And if you don't know what His will is, well, it has to line up with His Word in the Bible. I learned that and so much more by reading the King James Version of the Bible. When we do our will, we make mistakes, but bad choices can be corrected. With God's help, it can be done."

Kate nodded. "With God, all things are possible, Matthew 19:26."

"That scripture is why I'm excited to have this new beginning here at the farmhouse with you, and with my new job."

Kate pulled into the gas station to return the U-Haul and glanced at Gina.

"I think you are going to be fine. We both are. I'm going to run in and pay these people and drop this trailer."

"I enjoyed our talk." Gina stated.

"Me too. I've got a feeling it's the first of many."

Chapter Twenty-Five

Octavia released the button on the desk phone. Douglas and Richard's remarks about a meth lab at the farmhouse sent cold chills through her.

Not only destroying Ethan and Kate's life but selling meth to others and ruining their lives as well.

That's not fair…Judy, Douglas, and Richard against Kate and Ethan Meyers…and then Douglas and Richard against Judy...what an evil mind planning all of that...

Richard emerged from his office and hurried past her desk.

"Oh, thanks for working late.

You can go now. I'll close up."

"Thank you, Mr. Bailey. I do have errands to run."

"Go ahead. I'll see you in the morning."

She removed her purse from the desk drawer and yanked her car keys out of it. Without another glance at her boss, she went out the office door.

Octavia drove straight to the Crockett Police Department. Parking behind the building, she hurried on the sidewalk to the entrance. She rushed inside and looked around.

An officer behind a bulletproof glass window looked at her in the small, isolated room she found herself in. Several cameras were on her. He spoke into a microphone.

"Hello. Please identify yourself and tell me the nature of your visit."

"I'm Octavia Leigh, and I need to talk to a detective."

"Ma'am, can you tell me what this is about?"

"No sir, I'd rather not. It is important though."

"One moment. I'll have a detective come down and talk to you."

"Thank you."

There were no chairs in the tiny room. Octavia stood rooted to the ground. Not one to slouch, she held herself straight without leaning against the wall. She caught herself wringing her hands and suddenly stopped.

"Ms. Leigh?" An officer emerged from an opening door as a loud buzzer went off. He addressed her in a kindly manner.

"Yes."

"I'm Ira Pascal. I'll evaluate your concerns and request a detective if I decide one is needed." He smiled. "It's just a procedure, ma'am. We'll talk at my office where you don't have to stand."

He nodded at the officer in the glassed-in area and the buzzer went off again as the door opened.

Octavia followed him down a hallway and into an office.

"Please have a seat." He motioned to the two chairs in front of the desk and immediately sat in the one behind it.

"Do you mind if I record you? Saves a lot of time and is more accurate at details than my memory." He smiled again.

"No, that's fine."

He turned the recorder on and glanced at her. "For the record, please state your name, and I'll give mine with the time and date."

"I'm Octavia Leigh." Her voice broke and she inhaled deeply.

"Are you okay with this interview?" Mr. Pascal inquired softly and turned the recorder off.

"Yes, I'm nervous but I want to continue." She flashed a wide smile at him.

"Okay, Ms. Leigh. Let's start over."

Turning on the recorder, he addressed her again.

"For the record, please state your name, and I'll give mine with the time and date."

"I am Octavia Leigh."

"And I am Ira Pascal. I'm recording both of us. It is 6:45 pm on the first day of October 2017. Ms. Leigh, will you state why you are here?"

She leaned forward. "Yes, sir. I work for an attorney, a local attorney, and he is involved in something illegal."

"How do you know this, Ms. Leigh?"

"I overheard my boss on the phone."

"So, you were eavesdropping?" Ira Pascal lowered his voice.

"Well, no, I mean, it didn't start out like that."

"Ms. Leigh, take your time and start from the beginning." He advised.

"The other day, I accidentally left the intercom on, and couldn't believe Mr. Bailey's conversation with a new client, Douglas Futrell. It shocked and upset me. I had no choice but to listen. Mr. Futrell isn't his correct name, Mr. Bailey had it changed to Futrell so the local people wouldn't recognize him."

She paused and looked straight at Ira Pascal. "They have a woman, Judy Harris, who is destroying the reputation of Ethan and Kate Meyers so that Mr. Bailey and Mr. Futrell can take the farmhouse away from the Meyers. They are going to prove Mr. Futrell is the owner of the property, and after Judy Harris convinces the town to be on her and Mr. Futrell's side, Mr. Bailey told Mr. Futrell to get rid of her."

"That is some story, Ms. Leigh. I personally know Richard Bailey and can't see why he would do anything to jeopardize his license to practice law."

"He and Mr. Futrell are making plans with their contacts to have a meth lab out there. I forgot to tell you that I looked at Mr. Futrell's file and he has recently been paroled from prison."

Ira glanced at her, narrowing his eyes. "Has this Douglas Futrell talked to you in passing while going to see Richard?"

"He flirts, but I don't have anything to do with him."

"And Richard Bailey, how does he treat you?"

"Mr. Bailey is professional and treats me as a professional simply there to work. Mr. Pascal…" She frowned and had a tightness to her face as she paused. "I wouldn't be here if it wasn't important. When this becomes public; I'll be fired before Mr. Bailey loses his license to practice law, and there goes my job. I don't care, though. This is an evil plan they have against the Meyers."

"Excuse me, Ms. Leigh." He rose

from his chair and spoke over the recorder. "For the record, myself, and the other deputy being Caleb Davis, took the criminal mischief call at the Meyers farmhouse when they first arrived here from Houston."

He shut the recorder off and muttered something under his breath.

Crossing his arms tightly over his chest, he spoke in a quiet voice.

"I believe you, Ms. Leigh, and for two reasons. One, you are right, your job will be history, and two, it explains the gossip even I have heard about the Meyers."

He buzzed someone on his phone and clenched his jaw.

"Can you meet me in my office, right away? Thanks."

An older officer arrived, and Mr. Pascal withdrew the tape from the recorder. "Here, take this to Judge Quinn and tell him we need a wiretap order for Bailey, Futrell, and Harris. Oh, and make us a copy before you give this to him. I want to know as soon as we can set this wiretap up."

The officer left with the tape recording and Mr. Pascal turned to face Octavia Leigh.

"Young lady, you don't have to listen to Bailey or Futrell anymore. Don't want you getting caught anyway. We'll have the wiretap installed and recorded for evidence. I agree, and I know the judge will also, that you did the right thing. Go to work as if nothing happened, and we'll be building a case. Oh, and if you are interested, we do have an opening here for a dispatcher. You seem to be a caring person, and people call 911 for help. Think about it. You'd do well at the job."

"Thank you, sir, for believing me, and yes, I will consider the job."

He escorted her out of the police station and shut the buzzing door behind her.

Octavia walked around the building to her parked vehicle. Glancing up at the sky, she briefly closed her eyes, and let out a huge breath.

Thank You, Lord Jesus…

Chapter Twenty-Six

Kate drove as the morning sun rays slipped through the treetops. Gina sat beside her, dressed in a light blue wrap-around dress with mid-length sleeves.

"Such a bright day to start a new job. By the way, that color is becoming on you." Kate glanced at her new friend with a thoughtful expression.

"Thanks for letting me borrow it. I've always been partial to blue."

A plane flying overhead caught Elsa's attention as it made a circle in the sky. She leaned to the side it circled on. Kate glanced at her in the rear-view mirror and chuckled.

"Your daughter is certainly alert. She never misses a thing going on."

"She is that, and she remembers things I have to stop and recall. I plan on working hard and saving as much as I can for her. I'm determined she will get a college education."

"Well deserved goal for both of you." Kate nodded. "Neither Ethan nor I have children. We discussed adopting in the near future…" Her voice choked on the words. She shook her head. "I have to stop that. I'm praying and staying positive about Ethan's future now." She attempted to smile, and her face twitched.

Gina reached over and patted her shoulder.

Kate sighed. "I can't wait to see Ethan this morning."

Traffic increased and a car passing Kate shot by accelerating even faster as it switched lanes and almost sideswiped another vehicle ahead of Kate.

"You're too fast, buddy. You can have the whole road, and we'll all park." She exclaimed with a frown.

"That's telling him, Kate." Gina laughed.

"No, that's not right. Forgive me Lord." Kate sputtered. "I am only cranky if I don't get enough sleep. I do try to bite my tongue though. Nowadays I'm terrified of road rage. If that driver were close to me, I promise you I'd do nothing to make him notice me. Some places are having drive-by shootings for less than that happening."

"It's getting scary. Being courteous definitely needs to make a comeback."

"Amen to that."

Kate took the exit to Jarmann's Market and arrived a few minutes early. Gina lifted Elsa from her car seat and turned to wave at Kate.

"Be careful and call me if you need me."

"Thanks, Gina, I will, and you enjoy your day."

Gina nodded and entered the store.

Kate prayed half-aloud while traveling to the hospital. With the passing of each mile, she felt her faith and strength grow stronger.

She parked her car under shade trees and enjoyed the morning breeze gently blowing her hair as she strolled through the parking lot.

Entering the hospital, she avoided the two staff workers at the front information desk and went straight to the elevator. A short wait, and the elevator doors opened. A nursing aid with a cart full of supplies waited for her to enter, then the aid left scurrying away huffing as she pushed the heavy-laden cart down the hallway.

Kate made her way to Room 317 and stopped when she saw him. Alone in the room, he lay still amongst tubes to his mouth, tubes to his chest, hooked up to a machine, and a monitor. His I.V. had been changed from his right arm to his left hand. Kate glanced at the top of the I.V. pole and counted four various sizes of clear plastic bags containing liquid medicines. The large bag of saline shriveled with little fluid left in it. She hurried to his side and gasped.

His face needed shaving. With his hair in disarray, and by the body odor, he had obviously not been given a bath.

Yes, he is on a ventilator, and yes, he is unconscious, but he is a person. No one should be neglected like that…and they are not short-handed from what I've seen…

Kate noticed loose tubing connectors and small paper packages ripped open and discarded on the floor. Another look and she discovered the full trash can.

She reached over and caressed his cheek gently with her hand. The stubble scratched her skin, and she slowly continued anyway.

Ethan is a well-groomed man, he would be appalled at his current condition, critical or not.

She stopped and noticed again the many deep bruises on his hands and arms.

How many times did they miss the vein in trying to insert the IV? Does he have rolling veins? They didn't allow me in here, I don't know what happened…

She shook her head in agony and prayed again.

Dear God, I pray for healing and comfort for this man, if it be Your will, please heal him, if his time here is over, please don't let him suffer. Lord, be with him, surround him with Your love, and hold him in

Your arms. In Jesus' Holy name, I pray, Amen.

Kate smoothed Ethan's tangled hair the best she could with her fingers. She wiped her silent tears and sat beside him in a chair. Gazing at the machines, she watched the numbers change on his monitor and rushed to his side again. One machine began pumping, and the numbers jumped higher, then lower. Kate found part of the call cord for the nurse. Tangled in the padding, it had fallen to the bottom of the mattress. She jerked it loose and clicked the button.

"Yes?" A nurse asked with obvious surprise.

"My husband's monitor has numbers that are rapidly changing."

"But it's not beeping, ma'am. We are aware of his monitor. The doctor will be making his rounds soon. He'll talk to you then." She ended the call.

Being careful to not touch the IV tubing taped to his hand, Kate lightly touched the bruised puffy top of his hand with her fingertips.

"Ethan, Ethan, can you hear me? Bend your fingers if you can hear me."

He never moved. No eyelids fluttered. No difference in his breathing.

Kate caressed his cheek again as he remained unconscious.

A knock on the door disturbed her thoughts, and she turned to see a doctor with a nurse beside him.

"Mrs. Meyers?"

"Yes."

"I'm Dr. Grant, and this is the charge nurse, Mrs. Russell. May we speak to you in the hall?"

"Yes, of course."

Another nurse entered and checked the drip on the IV as they walked out.

"I'm afraid there is nothing more we can do for your husband. The tests we took earlier came back showing no brain activity."

Tears slipped from Kate's eyes as she silently stared at the doctor.

"I took the liberty to read his Texas driver's license for information and he is listed as an organ donor. We will need to decide soon. I realize this is a shock to you, but unfortunately, he did have a massive heart attack."

"It all happened so fast. This shouldn't be happening to him."

"I understand, and you do have our sympathies."

"I…I know he would want to donate and be of help to someone. Go ahead and make the arrangements."

"We'll have to take him off the ventilator. He could pass away quickly or last for a few days."

"If you are certain there is no brain activity."

"The tests are positive. I am sorry."

"Then go ahead and do it."

"I'll need you to sign these permission papers for the organ donations, and a team is on standby waiting to begin. You realize he did give his body to science."

Kate nodded solemnly, glancing at each page as she signed her name.

The nurse left instantly with the papers, and quickly returned without them.

"The team has been informed."

Dr. Grant nodded at the nurse, and she removed the breathing apparatus covering Ethan's mouth. Quietly, she pulled the ventilator's plug from the wall removing all electric current from operating the machine.

Ethan passed away immediately. The sudden straight

line on his EKG monitor confirmed it.

Kate stared at the monitor and absentmindedly put both hands over her mouth and screamed. Her screaming stopped as the nurse escorted her from Ethan's room, and into the doctor's office a few doors down, but her hands remained in front of her mouth.

Mrs. Russell gave Kate a bottle of cold water and had her drink it. Kate sobbed between gulps and hung her head.

"I can't believe he's gone." Kate stammered and tried to wipe away her tears, but they kept coming.

"I am so sorry, Mrs. Meyers. Is there anyone I can call for you?"

"No, not right now. Thank you."

"We'll collect his belongings and have them ready for you this afternoon, or whenever you are ready to get them. The donor recipients' families have requested to pay for Mr. Meyers' memorial. Do you want to use the local funeral home?"

"They did? Yes, the one here. And you have my phone number?"

"Yes ma'am. Are you sure you are okay to drive home?"

"Yes."

They turned to leave the doctor's office as several men wearing white lab coats entered Room 317.

Kate caught her breath and rushed out of the hospital with a hand covering her mouth again. Outside, her sobs racked her body, and she hurried to the car. Slipping behind the steering wheel, she moaned.

"Oh, Ethan. Ethan, Ethan, Ethan."

Her sobs lessened and she gazed at the sky.

"I should be happy for you, Ethan. You are with our Father in Heaven right now. You are getting to praise God in person."

Sitting in the car she quietly scanned the parking lot while tears intermittently rolled down her face. People were coming and going from their vehicles as she painfully watched. The sudden rising and falling of her chest continued as her thoughts were flooded with Ethan.

How can people walk about as if everything's the same? Don't they know Ethan is gone? Don't they know my whole world is shattered? They get out of their cars and couples hold hands, laughing as they hurry through the parking lot. Oh, I can't stand to look at them…it hurts too much without Ethan…

She sighed loudly.

But I can't begrudge them their time together, Ethan and I had ours…

Wiping her eyes again, she put the Chevy in reverse and paused.

I have to call Sal and Maria…and get Pastor Williford in Houston…and tell Gina…

Positioning the car into drive, she glanced at the parking lot, and then at the sky again.

Oh, Ethan…who would have thought… from our group evacuating Houston…that I'd be the only one to live in the farmhouse…

She choked back a sob and drove off.

At the farmhouse, she set the alarm for four o'clock to get Gina from the market by five. Tears sprang up again. Exhausted, she fell across the bed and cried into her pillow. Her harsh cries turned into soft whimpering and finally, she fell asleep.

The noise of someone knocking forcefully on the front door woke her.

Dazed, Kate glanced out the window.

How strange…a police officer…

She edged to the living room and jerked the door open.

"Mrs. Meyers? Mrs. Kate Meyers?"

"Yes." She narrowed her eyes at him with no regard to her disheveled appearance. "Mr. Leming, isn't it?"

Officer Daniel Leming reeled back upon seeing her bloodshot eyes and swollen tear-stained face.

"Yes, Mrs. Meyers. Are you alright?"

"No, no I'm not. My husband died this morning."

"I am so sorry. Please accept my condolences and my apologies for intruding on you today. Unfortunately, I have to serve you with papers, legal papers for you to appear in court. You will need to obtain an attorney."

"I don't understand. I just signed papers at the hospital."

Officer Leming lowered his voice to a soft gentle tone.

"Mrs. Meyers, you are being sued. Mr. Douglas Futrell has hired Mr. Richard Bailey as his attorney. He claims he is the legal owner of your husband's property."

Kate's mouth fell open, and she tried to lift her puffy eyelids. "What? Who is he and how can he do this?"

"I'm not at liberty to discuss it at this time. Read these papers and obtain an attorney soon. I need you to sign this document stating you have been served."

He thrust the pen and page towards her, and she hesitated while clutching the pen.

"I realize you're only doing your job." Kate muttered.

She straightened her posture and after examining the document, she finally signed her name. "And they, Mr. Leming, will realize I won't be defeated."

She handed pen and paper back to him, and for the first time all day, she smiled.

"Thank you, Mrs. Meyers, and again, if there is any way I can help you, call."

She nodded at him as he left and returned inside the house.

"Suing me...oh the nerve..." Kate scoffed.

She splashed cold water on her face, brushed her hair and changed clothes as she fumed. Grabbing the dog leash, she took Rufus to the backyard to do his business. Afterward, he wanted to play, and she couldn't resist. A feeling of calmness drenched her, and she patted Rufus. Gazing into his happy face, she gently grabbed him and carried him back inside.

"If you ever get too big to be carried, that's where hugs come in." She hugged the little dog and removed the leash.

"Got to run, behave yourself."

Rufus barked at her as she gathered her purse and car keys.

Arriving at Jarmann's Market, Kate parked near the front entrance and waited on Gina and Elsa. She didn't have long to wait.

Karl walked Gina out to the car holding Elsa.

He opened the back car door for her, and together they placed Elsa in her car seat. Laughter erupted as Karl gave up on the straps. Gina took over and secured her daughter.

"Takes practice." Gina teased.

"I hope I get the chance to get it right." He grinned.

"I think it can be arranged." She adjusted the seat belt and shut the door.

"Dinner tonight?"

"Yes. I'd like that, Karl." Gina glanced at Kate. "That is if I can find a babysitter."

"Of course, you can. Elsa is no problem, and she'll start yawning around eight o'clock. We'll both be asleep before you return home."

"Thank you." Gina nodded at Kate.

Karl waved through the window at Elsa and turned toward Gina.

"Six o'clock be alright?"

"That'll work for me." Gina slipped into the passenger's seat and grabbed her seat belt.

"See you then." Karl shut Gina's car door and walked back to the store.

Kate drove back to the freeway as Gina jabbered about her day.

"I love my job. The day goes by so fast, and Karl's mother gets along great with Elsa. Can you believe I'm going on a dinner date? Me?" Gina laughed.

"I'm happy for you. And yes, I can believe the dinner date. Remember, I've seen how Karl looks at you."

"The attraction is mutual." Gina chatted.

"Gina, I have something to tell you, but not while I'm driving. Two things actually." Kate frowned and shot her a quick look.

Gina instinctively tensed and shifted in her seat.

"Oh, Kate. It's not Ethan, is it?"

Kate stared straight ahead, never taking her eyes off the road. "We'll talk as soon as we get home."

No one spoke the remainder of the way. Occasionally, Kate would try to smile at her, and Gina politely smiled back. They arrived at the farmhouse, and Gina sat Elsa on the floor with her baby dolls. Elsa squealed and held them together in her arms, talking to each one. Gina pulled up a chair and motioned for Kate to join her.

Kate appeared strained and unable to talk. She glanced at Gina and nodded.

"Ethan passed away this morning." She trembled and had to stop.

"Oh no. Oh, my heart aches for you, Kate. You two were so close."

"We were, and I keep telling myself he is in Heaven now. But I miss him. He had no..." She paused. "He had no brain activity. He lay in the hospital bed with uncombed hair and needing to shave. It's horrible seeing anyone helpless like that, especially being unconscious."

Kate burst into tears, and Gina jumped up and hugged her. They cried together, before returning to their chairs.

"Oh Kate, I would have been there with you if I had known."

"I didn't want to call you on your first day of work." Kate sputtered.

"It would have been fine."

"Ethan's Memorial Service will be at the local funeral home. Ethan believed in helping others, and as an organ donor, he's still helping. He also gave his body to science."

"He'll be giving the gift of life. That sounds like the Ethan I heard you talk about. I am sorry I never got to meet him."

"You would have liked him." Kate got up from her chair and paced. "Oh, and the other important thing; I had papers served on me today. And guess what? I'm being sued. Someone named Douglas Futrell claims he's the legal owner of mine and Ethan's property."

Gina jerked her head towards Kate. "Douglas? As in the Douglas I escaped?"

Kate stopped pacing and looked wide-eyed at Gina.

"I may be wrong, Kate, but I don't think this is a coincidence. My Douglas, and your Douglas, are somehow connected …"

Chapter Twenty-Seven

Pastor Williford stood at the podium in the funeral chapel. Pictures of Ethan Meyers were on the wall and displayed on easel stands behind him. With a forlorn expression on his face, he glanced once more at the double doors for anyone else who might arrive late.

No one else entered.

Row after row of empty pews seemed to be a testimony of what small-town gossip can do to anyone.

Pastor Williford's chest rose as he waited five more minutes but to no avail.

He cleared his throat.

"I have the honor of officiating the Memorial today for Ethan Herschel Meyers. For those of you who knew him, he will be greatly missed. For those of you who did not know him, I thank you for paying your respect. Usually, a memorial begins with the date of birth and when the deceased passed away. I'm not doing that though. I think there are more important points to make known about Ethan Meyers."

He paused and smiled at each of the ten people seated in the enormous room.

"Ethan didn't know he had heart trouble. He had a massive heart attack. He didn't know about the gossip concerning him and Kate. He didn't know Kate is being sued.

I mention this now because neither Ethan nor Kate deserved any of that kind of treatment. I can sum Ethan up in one sentence; serving God is everyone's number one purpose, and Ethan did that wholeheartedly. Everyone who knew Ethan, knew him to be a Christian man who believed in helping others and always sharing the gospel with them. He wanted all to receive salvation in Jesus Christ. If we are to learn anything from his legacy, it is the love and kindness he gave to all. If you needed a friend to talk to, you talked to Ethan. If he discovered you were hungry, groceries would be delivered to your home. If you lost your job, your home, your car, or whatever happened; Ethan would get on his phone and plan for a solution. I remember his favorite saying, 'We'll figure it out', and he'd tell you with God's help we will do it. You might sleep in his garage, or work at a temporary job he found, or donate your time to helping someone else while your car got repaired using the bartering method. His motto: 'Christians helping Christians helping to bring others to Christ.' That is the Ethan I knew."

He cleared his throat again and took a long drink from a water bottle.

"I feel led to bring everything out in the open concerning what happened to this fine Christian man. If you look around, you'll count ten people who are attending this Memorial. I am not judging, but do you realize this is Ethan's hometown?"

He walked in front of the podium and lowered his voice.

"I want to pray for the townspeople of Crockett who were led astray by gossip. I don't know if it began by brainwashing or by someone being conniving, but the wickedness spread. No, Ethan did not kill his first wife, and yes, he and Kate were married."

He momentarily held his arms in the air and his voice quivered. "Lord have mercy on the mind of a neighbor and the harm it caused. Whoever started it, whoever added to it, whoever got caught up in it; Lord, please have them remember the old saying, 'Birds of a Feather Flock Together.' They choose to remain with the evil group and continue to destroy reputations. Remind them of Your Word in the

Bible; 'Don't cast your pearls before swine.' Lord, we pray for those to repent and ask for forgiveness because we know they will have to answer to You for the way they treated Ethan and Kate. Lord, we pray for You to place Christians in their path to show them the way out of the Devil's darkness. Lord, we pray for their soul, and for them to know You as their Savior. In Jesus' Holy name, we pray, Amen."

He walked to the front pew where Kate sat and held her hand.

"Kate, we know Ethan is with our Heavenly Father. He is praising God and he is singing, and he is happy. I pray for God's peace that surpasses all understanding to overwhelm you, and I pray for your comfort, and your protection. In Jesus' Holy name, I pray, Amen."

Kate stood and faced the Pastor.

"I take comfort in knowing you can call Ethan, a saved man, a born-again Christian, and a new creature in Christ, and he did not suffer in the end. I couldn't be with him, but he knew how I felt. He knew my love." Her voice broke, but she continued. "I thank all of you for coming, and I want to introduce Pastor Williford to the others who are here." She turned and pointed to the three policemen sitting together.

"Ira Pascal, Caleb Davis, and Daniel Leming."

They shook hands with the Pastor and turned towards Kate.

"Ma'am, we are sorry for your loss. If we can be of any help, please don't hesitate to call. We are here to serve and protect."

Kate's eyes welled up with tears. "Thank you, and I am so grateful for what you do each and every day."

They solemnly nodded and left the chapel.

Sal, Maria, and their children Carlos and Rosa hurried to Kate and the Pastor and hugged them tightly.

"Sorry for the circumstances that brought us together." Pastor Williford told the Hernandez family.

"It seems surreal." Sal stated.

Carlos and Rosa encircled the Pastor's legs and hugged him with their small arms. He patted their heads and smiled at them.

"Hi, little ones. My goodness, you aren't so little anymore. You have grown taller since I've seen you."

"Mama cooks and we eat it." Carlos announced.

Maria laughed. "They have a good appetite."

Gina, Elsa, and Karl approached the group, and Kate met them with a tearful smile.

"Pastor Williford, this is Gina Sehlke and her daughter, Elsa, who live with me. And this is Gina's friend, Karl Schuhmacher."

"Nice to meet you. I'm glad Kate has friends here. She needs them now more than ever."

"Pastor, I'll be fine." Kate softly replied.

"Kate is a good person, we're here for her." Gina slipped her arm around Kate's waist.

Karl nodded, making eye contact with the Pastor.

"That is reassuring." Pastor Williford smiled at the couple.

Gina leaned toward the Pastor and spoke in a low, steady voice. "May I ask you something?"

"Yes, of course." He answered surprised.

"What does it mean, don't cast your pearls before swine?"

"It means don't offer something valuable or offer what you hold dear to someone who won't appreciate it. For example, yourself. You are valuable, and with someone who doesn't value your worth, you will be in a toxic situation. You will be stepped on and thrown away when they've used you all they can. That's why you stay away from them. They want to ruin you like they are ruined."

Gina shook her head. "It's sad when you recognize it happening to someone, and they are blind to it."

"Yes, it is. All we can do is pray for them."

Kate glanced at her watch. "Pastor, I don't want to interrupt but you are about to be late for your flight home."

"We'll drive you to the airport." Sal offered. "Where's your luggage?"

"It's in the office. I'll get it." He took off in a hurry.

"Nice to meet you." He called out to Gina and Karl.

"You too."

Gina hugged Kate again. "We'll see you later."

Kate smiled as Gina, Elsa, and Karl walked out of the chapel.

Pastor Williford returned with his luggage, and they all walked to the parking lot.

"We'll keep in touch, Kate. I'll be checking on you."

"Thanks again, Pastor. Love you."

"Love you, too."

He climbed into the Chisum work van that Sal drove, and he

and the Hernandez family waved to Kate as they left the parking lot.

Kate stood still and momentarily closed her eyes.

"Thank you, Lord, this whirlwind day is over, and thank you for my friends being here with me. Bless and protect them all. In Jesus' Holy name, Amen."

An employee of the funeral home caught her as she opened her car door.

"Mrs. Meyers, we'll bring Mr. Meyers pictures to your house tomorrow, if that will be convenient for you?"

"It will. Thank you."

She drove to the farmhouse alone with her thoughts. As soon as she parked in front of the house, little Rufus barked from inside the house in full guard dog mode. She laughed and let him out. Glad to see her, he ran around in a circle before jumping up on her legs, and she didn't want to go in.

No longer afraid, Kate remained outside letting Rufus run and play. Taking in the view of the pastures, the tall grass swayed in the distance. She could hear the soft shushing sound as the wind continued blowing across the surrounding acres.

Ethan should be enjoying this peacefulness with me…no, I can't start thinking like that…his time here is over and I'm glad for the time we had…and I know he's rejoicing and singing and praising God in Heaven…

Kate wiped tears from her face and wandered onto the front porch.

Sitting in one of the many wooden rocking chairs, she basked in the late afternoon sun. Rufus spotted her and darted up the steps. Excited to see her, he barked and wiggled happily. She bent forward and gently patted him until he curled up at her feet and fell asleep. Kate leaned back in the rocker experiencing waves of fatigue and blinked rapidly trying to stay awake, but wave after wave of sheer tiredness zapped her until she dozed off.

Karl and Gina arrived hours later and caught Kate and Rufus sleeping soundly on the porch.

"I hate to wake her, but it's almost dark. She needs to come in. They both do." Gina shook her head at them. "That is so sweet, Karl. Look at them."

He grinned. "Take a picture. She'll treasure it. Hurry."

Gina snatched her cell phone from her purse and took several pictures. The flash disturbed Rufus. He stood up on top of Kate's feet and she stirred in the rocking chair. Her eyes suddenly popped open as she gazed at Gina and Karl.

"Oh, I fell asleep." She yawned and glanced at them again.

"Where is Elsa?"

"She wanted to spend the night and Mom loves reading stories to her. When we left, Elsa had picked out two bedtime stories." Karl revealed. "Let's go inside. We brought pizza."

"Oh, how nice. What a great idea." Kate rose from the chair and carried Rufus in as Gina and Karl retrieved the pizza from his car.

"Karl also brought a gallon of iced tea. I'll get the glasses. Why don't you relax in the living room?"

"Okay. And thanks for everything."

Kate turned on the television and lounged in a loveseat. Karl and Gina passed out the food and drinks and eased onto the couch. Kate flipped through the channels and discovered her favorite show.

"Oh, I love Blue Bloods. Ethan and I always watched it." She smiled.

"We watch it at home too." Karl nodded.

"I haven't been able to see it for a long time. I feel like we need popcorn." She laughed.

Ten minutes into the program, an announcer interrupted as the words BREAKING NEWS flashed across the screen.

"An anonymous source provided evidence of fraud and an illegal narcotics scheme planned by three residents of Crockett, Kansas. Authorities have confirmed all three are in custody and are now being held in Shawnee County Jail in Topeka. Their pictures have been released. The first is Judy Harris, age 52 years old, held for fraud, stolen firearms, slander, and illegal narcotics possession. Douglas Futrell, age 53 years old, was held for fraud, a felony with stolen firearms, illegal narcotics possession, forging a legal instrument, slander, attempted 1st-degree murder, and armed robbery. Richard Bailey, a local attorney, age 57 years old, was held for fraud, stolen firearms, illegal narcotics possession, forging a legal instrument, and attempted 1st-degree murder. Details are forthcoming as the investigation continues. This has been breaking news on your CBS news channel and now we'll return you to your local scheduled program."

"That is the Douglas I knew." Gina gasped.

Karl bounced off the couch. "That's the guy who robbed us, Gina, the day we were to interview you. We had to keep it quiet, but we don't anymore. He presented himself as a police officer, uniform and all." His face flushed as he stared wide-eyed at the television screen.

"Wow! So that's the "Judy" who ruined mine and Ethan's reputation. And that's Douglas who planned on taking this property. Guess I'm no longer being sued. And that attorney, he won't be practicing law again." Kate shuttered.

"Nope. The truth comes out."

"I saw a police officer near the store the day of the scheduled interview. Oh, my...so that is Douglas clean-shaven." Gina shook her head. "I don't understand how they all got together. And why go after the Meyers?"

"They aren't through investigating. Wait, did you say you knew this guy Douglas, Gina?" Karl blurted.

"…Yes, unfortunately, I did. I'll explain it in the morning."

"Karl, Douglas happened upon Gina, and she is fortunate he didn't harm her. They were never a twosome. The twosome I can't get over is Judy and Douglas, they are like two ticks without a dog…or I should say two ticks looking for a dog. I can't get over this. Judy started out gossiping and ended up running with crooked men. Run with thugs, die a thug…or at least expect to become one. That's a shame, her mind really is messed up now." Kate ranted.

"Yeah, but not like it's going to be in jail." Karl added.

"And attempted murder. What is that all about?" Kate vented.

"They were planning on killing someone. Apparently, they have evidence." Gina shook her head again in disbelief.

"Well, I hope they pray to God and ask for forgiveness and are sincere about it. I pray they come to know Jesus as their Savior. I can't stand the thought of someone not having the chance to go to Heaven."

Karl looked at the cold pizza. "I agree, and Gina, you and I need to go to the police station in the morning and tell them what we know. It sounds like the three of them tattled on each other."

"It does, doesn't it?"

"Yes, ma'am, and I think we should all call it a night. I'm going home. I'll see you in the morning." He blew Gina a kiss and waved at Kate. They heard the front door open and shut. Kate automatically went to lock it as Karl drove off.

She turned from the door and looked at Gina. "Wonder what the town of Crockett thinks of me and Ethan now?"

Chapter Twenty-Eight

Gina awoke to a silent house. No one else seemed to be up and moving. Rufus didn't even bark to be let outside. She hurried to the bathroom and readied herself for the day. Dressed and groomed, she went down the hallway and veered toward the kitchen. At the door, she noticed Kate sitting at the table.

Kate unconsciously turned her wedding-ring round and round on her finger while her morning coffee sat; a full cup, not steaming…obviously cold and untouched. Gina entered the kitchen and noticed Kate flinched.

"Oh, Kate. I'm sorry I intruded on your quiet time. This has to be awful for you without Ethan."

Kate attempted to smile. "I miss him deeply." She sighed and rose from her chair. "And he wouldn't want me sitting all day thinking about him. You look nice."

"Thanks, and Ethan wouldn't want you to be idle either. He'd be glad you've got the farmhouse. It has a lot of potential. Karl will be here soon. How do you like my hair?" Gina raised her eyebrows at Kate and stood still.

"Turn around."

Gina swirled and remained serious.

"Very becoming. Looks neat and professional on top of your head, especially with the few wisps of curls hanging near your ears."

"Thanks. First impressions mean a lot, and I want to make a good one at the police station."

"You'll be fine. I can't wait to hear what they tell you."

"I can't either. They'll never expect to hear what Karl and I have to tell them. I'm glad Karl is going to be with me."

"Me too. And I think Karl is going to be wherever you are." Kate smiled.

"I feel like we've known each other forever." Gina beamed as she continued. "He's on my mind constantly."

Rufus suddenly started barking as they heard a vehicle approach.

"Must be Karl." Gina ran to the front door and peeped through the side window. "Yes, it's him alright. I'll tell him about my marriage, and being homeless, and all of it. I don't believe in keeping secrets from each other. He'll know everything before we get to the police station. Bye Kate."

Kate waved at her. "He'll understand. Just be yourself and try to relax."

Gina disappeared out the door, and Kate automatically sprang to lock it. Yawning, she returned to the kitchen for a refill and carried the coffee cup and Rufus outside. She sat in a rocking chair on the porch as Rufus did his business. He scampered about stopping to sniff shrubbery, and if he weren't a dog, he'd have said Kate appeared deep in her own thoughts.

She suddenly leaped from the chair spilling her coffee.

Hmm, what did Gina say? Potential…I'll have to check that out…

"Come on, Rufus, I want to google something."

She filled his food dish and gave him fresh water before making her way to the office on the second floor. As soon as the computer took her password, she hurried and typed 'Day Care Centers, Crocket, Kansas' into Google Search and waited.

"None found?" Kate mumbled aloud. "No wonder Gina couldn't find a babysitter. Hmm. Looks like I found a need here no one has filled."

She googled state requirements for opening a licensed daycare facility and scanned the article.

"Not bad, and I'd love having children here. I could do it."

Her phone rang and she took the call.

"Kate?"

"Yes?"

"This is Daniel Leming. I have good news for you. The judge issued dismissal papers on the pending lawsuit. Apparently, you are no longer being sued."

"Thanks, that is wonderful news. I've decided I'm going to open a daycare center here, and this is all the incentive I need to start."

"Good for you, and I can put posters in key areas in town when you're ready to advertise if you want to… with ads in the local paper …that is if you want me to help? I mean, I don't want to rush you, but I think you need a friend in this town."

"Daniel, as another friend, you would be welcome. I'm grieving for Ethan, and I will be. My only friends here are Sal and Maria, and Gina and Karl. I would be glad to call you one of my friends."

"Thank you, Kate, I know you are grieving, and I would never intrude. I'm sorry I didn't get to meet Ethan. From what I've heard, you were married to a good Christian man."

"Yes… but …how did you hear anything about him?"

"Oh, I forgot to tell you. Karl and Gina were at the station earlier, and we learned a lot from each other. They listened to recorded tapes from all three arrested in the case, and they told us the rest of it. I called to say it's over, and you don't have to appear in court. Karl and Gina said to tell you they'll go on to work and see you this afternoon. They sure seem like a nice couple."

"They are. And what a relief Douglas' plan failed. I'm glad all of you got together."

"Yes, and Kate, do you realize this started with Judy's gossip? Then Douglas played her, and between her medicine for being bipolar and whatever else he gave her, she may not have been aware of…well…her mind is gone. Her brain is fried."

"No, I didn't. I have to admit I did have trouble forgiving, especially the gossip, that's what kept me from being with Ethan. The gossip could have had some bearing on the care he received, I'll never know. I don't even know how many or how few hours he had of being conscious or unconscious, but I prayed about it, and I do forgive everyone involved. I forgive them so God will forgive me of my own sins, and I even pray for my enemies to know Jesus Christ as their Savior."

"Your enemies?"

"Yes, the townspeople of Crockett."

"Kate, they aren't your enemies anymore. Maybe one day soon you'll visit my church and I'm sure you'll find out what I'm talking about."

"Okay, I will. Meanwhile, I'll picture the daycare center in full swing, and eventually see a yellow school bus driving down my long driveway bringing kids here after school."

"It's a start."

"Yes, you're right, Daniel." Kate sighed. "I guess I'd better let you get back to work."

"Wait. Don't you want my home phone number?"

"I'd like that."

He gave it to her, and she jotted it down.

"Thanks, Daniel."

"Yes, ma'am, as I said, it's a start."

"Yes, it is." Kate smiled to herself as they ended the call.

The End

About the author:

I am blessed to have 2 married sons who are both Christians, as are their immediate families. Both are busy but so reliable when I need them! It's nice to have someone call and check on you! My daughters-in-law are as kind and thoughtful as my sons are. I have one grandson who will be a pilot with the USAF commissioned as a 2nd Lieutenant when he graduates from Texas A&M this year! I treasure the videos I have of the four years of him being a Corps of Cadets member; all the marching and drills! I have one granddaughter who is like the daughter I never had, and along with her husband, have just given me my first great-grandchild! I also treasure videos of her with her Etsy business; she is so talented!

I am the only caregiver to my 94 yr. old mother who has Alzheimer's and dementia and a term new to me; it's called Sun Downers. They change when the sun goes down to an entirely different person. She lives with me and keeps me busy. She was sleepwalking, even falling in the dark, etc. but I now have a hospital bed for her with guard rails and a bed alarm. I highly recommend both. The times when she is herself and says "I love you" or "Thank you, you are so sweet" makes it all worthwhile. It is so sad to see her look at me for help when she doesn't understand something. I center everything around her and although it may take longer to do; I have many interests I also enjoy.

I've always loved writing, and I now write in bits and spurts: writing notes and ideas while on the run…

whenever I can. I have started writing on my next book. It will be a stand-alone book in regular print, and I am excited to see it completed. Look for it in the coming year.

I recently began growing vegetables using the hydroponic method. It is really hot here in Texas with a drought and a brown, crunchy lawn in the summer. Plants do not have a chance! So, I'm enjoying growing my "garden" inside. So far, so good! I even have indoor fruit trees that are self-fertile.

And more importantly, I am a Christian learning about God's eternal Torah, that is God's instructions for us and learning His festivals. It is really increasing my walk with the Lord, and I have never had more peace and joy.

Last but not least, I enjoy my little Yorkie dogs. They put themselves to bed at night, and then bark at me to come and shut their kennel doors. Cletus, LeRoy, and Tinkerbell. Since she is the only female of the Yorkies, I nicknamed her Doggie Girl. She rounds out the family. They all relax with me when I'm in the recliner. One sprawls across my feet, one between me and the armrest, and one lays in my lap rolled over for a belly rub! So is the life of this writer. ☺

Other Books by Lynn Hobbs:

Running Forward Series: a
powerful faith and family saga,

[each published in regular print]

Book 1 - Sin, Secrets, and Salvation

Dave Penleigh belittled his wife Susan until she could no longer tolerate the mental abuse. A Christian wife, unequally yoked with a non-Christian husband; the only unshakeable part of her existence is her deep faith in God, which sustains her despite the trials she faces. Determined to be a survivor, she rebuilds her life with gusto. Unusual events occur. Is someone stalking her? Scripture, prayer, and intrigue round out this Christian suspense novel of Susan and her family.

Won 1st place in Religious Fiction by the Texas Association of Authors, 2013.

Book 2 - River Town

A powerful faith and family saga continues; inspiring, suspenseful, action-packed. Susan Penleigh relocates to Texas in 2011 during the worst drought in history with terrifying wildfires, a new job at a high school, and many people to challenge her faith. From troubled teenagers to an arrogant boss, scripture helps a woman's journey through modern family issues. A compelling page turner that will enthrall both men and women.

Won 1st Place in Religious Fiction by the Texas Association of Authors, 2014.

Book 3 - Hidden Creek

Two women, two men, fight the wages of sin. Who heals? Who follows God's will? Four journeys, four friends, turn the page, let the story begin. Suspense builds as new faces emerge. Unexpected surprises, exciting twists and turns, and lessons learned make Susan's world come alive. Through many struggles, does Susan's faith prevail? Will this family ever bond together? This book concludes the Running Forward Series.

Won 1st Place in Religious Fiction by the Texas Association of Authors, 2015.

Biography:

Lillie, A Motherless Child

This is the true-life story of Lillie Fritsche, born in Texas during the Great Depression era with 16 siblings. Lillie's mother passed away when Lillie was 7 years old. Follow the journey from a motherless child to an inspiring woman of faith. Large print, complete with treasured photos and handed down family recipes. Lillie is this author's own mother.

Won 1st place in Biography by The Texas Association of Authors, 2016.

[published in large print with pictures]

The American Neighborhood Series: this Christian fiction series also consists of three books. The reader can expect to find real life situations that will be surprising. Morals. No profanity, or violence, but neither do they follow "cookie cutter" plots. Boy may meet girl and marry girl, but typical, romantic, happy endings are not always guaranteed.

[each published in large print]

Book 1- Eyes of a Neighbor

You are introduced to a community with its residents of newcomers, and those who have lived most of their lives in this older, historical section of Houston, Texas. Kate Davis, a Hurricane Katrina survivor from Louisiana, inherits her late aunts' home and sees everything going on in the neighborhood. She lives across the street from Ethan and Becky Meyers, who recently left Kansas. The residents include all age groups and become tangled in a murder mystery. Suspense, intrigue, inspiration, and romance intertwine to create a fast passed read that is indeed a page turner.

Book 2- Heart of a Neighbor

Hurricane Harvey has formed in the Gulf of Mexico. Size and speed are increasing. Can Kate convince her neighbors in Houston to evacuate as it nears? Who goes? Who remains, and what awaits them? Will Richard want to know Jesus as his Savior? Heart-warming. Church family bonding. No profanity.

Book 3- Mind of a Neighbor

Trust builds as neighbors leave the disaster of Hurricane Harvey together. Faith is tested as they relocate to Kansas. Locals stir up sinister rumors that develop into unexpected trouble. Gossip abounds.
Can Ethan and Kate obtain God's peace that surpasses all understanding?
Can Kate forgive an entire town? Whose faith will remain true, and who is the neighbor with the evil mind?

Although *Mind of a Neighbor* is fiction, the struggles of the characters are very real.

An inspiring ending is **always** possible in any situation … when you know the promises of God have been given to see us through this evil world - and they always do! Yes… and Amen!

Enjoy this final book in the American Neighborhood Series.

A word from the publisher:

LIKE THE BOOK?

HELP THE AUTHOR!

REVIEWS HELP WITH FUTURE
SALES!

GIVE A REVIEW ON
AMAZON.COM

Did you know?

Most authors are not rich. In fact, most make less than $10,000 a year. Being an author is a small business.

If there are 50 reviews, Amazon lists a book in its newsletters and other promotions. They also will begin recommending the book to others as they browse books to purchase.

REVIEWS are the easiest way to say THANK YOU to the author and to tell their publisher to produce more books.

SUPPORT AUTHORS
SUPPORT SMALL BUSINESS

What to do?!?

1. Go to Amazon.com
2. In the Search Bar, type the book title and the Author's name. Example: Mind of a Neighbor Lynn Hobbs
3. Find the Book Title in the results
4. Click the hyperlink that says "Customer Reviews"
5. Click the hyperlink that says "Write a Customer Review"
6. Click the number of STARS you want as a rating. (5 is the BEST!)
7. Type in the comment area to write your review. It can be short and sweet, or an in-depth analysis of the book.

A good review is like gold to an author. If you have ever bought anything on Amazon, you automatically have an account, and can write a review. Reviews are sincerely appreciated!

-Thank you
Proof Productions